"Ground Zero:

A Zombie Apocalypse"

Nicholas Ryan

2

Prologue.
The Wrath.

The skyline of Baltimore hunched low on the horizon, appearing from out of the ocean in a silhouette of gleaming towers above a blanket of grey morning haze.

Behrouz Asgari stood by the freighter's starboard rail and stared towards the city. He had been watching since dawn, waiting for this moment.

Waiting for his first sight of the accursed place.

He had sensed the land – felt its vast restless presence in the darkness, tasted the scent of its corruption and greed on the breeze, like a fetid cloying tang in the back of his throat.

"I see you, great Satan," he muttered softly, his voice edged with the intensity of his hatred. "And there will be no escape from the Wrath I bring."

He glanced at his wristwatch and headed to his cabin. The freighter was scheduled to dock at noon, but he knew not to trust local authorities to maintain the schedule. No, he must wait until the last possible moment. His trainers had been clear on this matter. He had to be certain the ship was well within the harbor before he could take the final step.

His sleeping quarters was a narrow cramped space the size of a prison cell, with bunk beds fixed to one wall and a small chest of drawers in a corner. Asgari dropped onto the bottom bunk and stared at the walls. Beyond the open door he could hear the sounds of the ship slowly coming alive; crewmen shuffling along the narrow corridors in heavy boots and hard hats and bright colored safety vests.

He closed his eyes, and drew a deep steadying breath. The sounds around him faded. The tension seeped from his body as though he were meditating, until his mind and imagination filled with flashing memories of the makeshift camp back in the hot wastelands west of Kashan.

He remembered the Russian who had come, driven through the desert in a motorcade escorted by six trucks of elite Quds Force operatives. And he remembered the experiments the scientist had conducted on captured Iraqi soldiers – and the terrible madness that had infected them before their extermination.

He remembered watching the bloody horror on the prisoner's faces as they died and then re-awakened into something hideous and vicious and inhuman – and how the Quds troopers had used fire, and then acid, and finally a hail of bullets to the head before the ghouls had finally dropped dead in their iron cages and lay still.

Asgari smiled. Then his thoughts drifted to the defining moment of his life – the moment he had been driven through the cool night to a desert place south and east of Tehran where he had met the Supreme Iranian Leader, and been shown one of the vast underground bunkers that would be the new birthplace from which Islam would rise up victorious after the apocalypse.

Asgari had wept with pride when the Supreme Leader had told him that it was his calling to be Allah's final martyr, and that his place in Paradise would be assured, for he would be exalted as the greatest of all warriors.

"God has ordained you as the weapon of his fury," the Supreme Leader had declared solemnly. The old man's voice shook with passion as he took Asgari's hands within his own. "You will slay the infidel by the thousand, as a panther amongst fat listless sheep – and each drop of blood you draw will be celebrated in heaven."

Asgari opened his eyes suddenly and stared at the cabin wall, surprised to find that his vision was misted with fresh tears at the memory. There was a swelling lump of pride in his throat.

The Koran promised a Paradise of green land, flowing streams, fruit, wine and beautiful women, and his place there would be certain – for surely if those who had martyred themselves in the blast of a suicide bomb were walking in the gardens of paradise, then what greater reward would Allah bestow upon the believer who brought death upon *two hundred million* of the hated Americans?

Asgari reached down and unfastened the laces of one heavy work boot. There was a pocketknife in one of the dresser drawers and he used it to lever the heel off, holding the boot carefully in his lap. Beneath the cover, protected by thick black rubber padding, was an aluminum vial, as thick as a cigarette but only half as long. The cylinder was sealed in shrink-wrapped plastic. Asgari set the vial carefully on the mattress beside him. Then he refitted the heel and put the boot back on.

He glanced at his wristwatch. It was almost eleven am. He could feel the ship's motion changing as she nosed her way carefully into Baltimore harbor surrounded by attending tugboats. The rolling pitch became more gradual and the sound of the ship's engine throbbed and vibrated harshly up through the steel floor. Asgari leaned back against the cold wall and watched the time slowly tick away.

He wondered where it would begin. The Russian had assured him the dose was small enough to allow his spirit time to reach heaven before the Wrath would come upon his body – and Asgari believed the scientist. He had seen the effects of infected bites at the training camp, and had noted the re-awakening rage had taken only minutes to make the Iraqi prisoners rise again and turn them insane with the madness.

Asgari wondered whether his dead body would be taken to a hospital once they discovered him. Or perhaps he would be left lying cold on his bunk. That thought made him pause. He frowned for a moment.

Did it matter?

He didn't think so, but to be certain there would be no unnecessary delay transporting his corpse into the city, he took the counterfeit Egyptian passport and documents he had been issued in Tehran, and tucked them into his shirt pocket.

He smiled again, for by the time his body was found, he – Behrouz Asgari – would be in Paradise, and the terrible thing that remained of him would arise and be unstoppable.

He broke the plastic seal and unscrewed the tiny cap of the vial. His hands shook with the thrill of his anticipation. He recited random extracts from the Koran, coming back again and again to the one passage that resonated like a drumbeat in his heart.

"Kill the aggressors wherever you find them. Drive them out of the places from which they drove you..."

Finally he felt at peace. He muttered a last silent prayer, then closed his eyes and drank the virus. Then he swallowed the empty aluminum tube.

Asgari felt nothing for long moments, and then a sudden heavy weight of drowsiness forced him back down on the bunk. He sighed. He thought of his home in Iran as he patiently waited to die – and then rise again as the deadly Wrath of Allah.

For God had willed it to be so.

One.
The Infection.

Arthur Harrigan died because he was old and cautious.

Since his wife Martha had passed away, Arthur had lived a lonely, solitary life.

He kept to himself. He stayed around the house. Every weekend he went out into the garden and did battle with the rose bushes, and once a week his daughter in New York phoned to make sure he was still alive and not laying dead and maggot-infested on the kitchen floor.

On Thursday morning Arthur shuffled into the living room and switched on the television, then pulled the curtains open and stared out across the lawn.

Beyond his front fence, the world was going about its business; Mrs. Jamieson was standing by her mailbox chatting to the postman, and Doug Garvey was walking his dog. Arthur hated Garvey's little mutt, and if it crapped on the sidewalk out front of his house once more he was going to give the man a piece of his mind. He watched silently until the wretched little flee-bag had passed by his driveway, and then let the dusty curtains fall back into place.

Arthur sighed. He was old-man weary, with the kind of aches and pains that made every movement a slow deliberate effort of will.

He tottered to the big recliner and sat down with a heavy groan. The coffee table was in front of him. He stared down at the chess board and made a face. Bobby Fischer's *My 60 Memorable Games'* was lying open on the table. He picked the book up and snatched his spectacles from his cardigan pocket. Perched the glasses on the end of his nose and tried yet again to understand why Fisher had played his pawn to f4. He re-read the enigmatic Grandmaster's cryptic annotation for the move, and shook his head in complete bewilderment.

The mid morning news bulletin was on in the background and something unsettling in the tone of the presenter's voice instinctively compelled Arthur to look up sharply from the chess book and stare with rheumy eyes.

" – *stage authorities have no explanation for the outbreak,*" the grey-suited TV announcer was saying, his face dark and deeply concerned. "*All we can confirm at the moment is that Baltimore's hospital system has been inundated with patients – as many as one hundred and fifty at this stage – all seemingly presenting to medical staff with the same symptoms.*"

Arthur set the book down in his lap and frowned. He felt suddenly uneasy. He used the remote to turn up the television volume.

"*We're crossing now to Baltimore General Hospital, and we also have a reporter standing by in Atlanta where the Director of Research at the Centre for Disease Control is preparing to make a statement to the media,*" the TV anchor explained. "*We'll cross there live as soon as the press conference starts. In the meantime, here's Carrie Sullivan with a report from Baltimore General...*"

The image flickered, and then switched from the studio to a young blonde reporter who was standing on a strip of green lawn out front of a vast concrete building. In the background, two ambulances suddenly came into camera shot, their lights flashing and sirens wailing as they braked hard out front of the hospital's emergency entrance. The woman reporter winced at the sound and glanced over her shoulder at the vehicles, then turned quickly back to the camera. Her face was flushed with hectic color, and her voice was wavering as she began her report.

"John, the scene here is one of utter panic," the woman reporter spoke quickly. *"A fleet of ambulances have been arriving at the hospital since earlier today, and the entire hospital has been shut down and quarantined, on the orders of local authorities. That means no visitors allowed inside the building – and no one allowed out. It's... it's really quite frightening..."*

Arthur sat silently and stared at the television. The book slid from his lap but he didn't notice. All his attention was on the images flickering across the screen. Overlaid above the woman reporter's voice, the TV station was playing pre-recorded footage taken earlier in the day, which showed a horde of blood-covered people on the streets of Baltimore, staggering towards two police cars. Three cops were behind the vehicles. They had their weapons raised. The crowd staggered closer, walking trance-like, as though they were dazed and wounded.

Then the camera zoomed in close on a single man in the crowd. His eyes were wide and crazed. His unshaven face was a mask of blood, his shirt torn and gore-spattered. His mouth was open, lips snarled back so that his teeth were bared into a vicious, maddened growl. Arthur heard one of the cops in the foreground, shouting in panic. *"Stand still! Get on the ground!"*

He shouted again, this time his voice strident and more desperate. *"Get on the fuckin' ground!"*

One of the cops was holding a Remington 870 shotgun in the low-ready position. He was a big man, maybe in his mid forties. He was solid across the chest and shoulders. He had steady eyes – the steely gaze of a man who had seen enough on the streets not to be easily rattled. He pumped the action of the weapon and the menacing *clack-clack* sounded like an ominous warning.

The crowd came closer.

Suddenly there was a deafening roar, as the officers opened fire simultaneously on the shambling man. The camera shook again. Arthur thought he could hear someone weeping. Then the lens focused onto the dead man's body – just in time to see him get slowly back to his feet. There was thick brown ooze seeping from huge ragged holes that had ripped his chest apart.

Arthur Harrigan stopped breathing.

"Jesus wept," he gasped.

The cops fired again, and the blood-covered crowd around the downed figure suddenly erupted in a moan; a sound that was without form or coherence – but a wail so chilling and so demented that one of the policemen turned away and fled. The camera caught the horror on his face, the cop's jaw hanging slack, his ashen features twisted and contorted with fear and panic. Arthur heard a voice off-camera shout, *"Run for your fuckin' life!"* and then the picture began to jerk and bounce. He could hear ragged breathing as the footage tilted at crazy angles, showing crowds of screaming, fleeing people, rushing in a chaotic mass of panic. He could hear car alarms in the background and the heavy thump of a helicopter's rotors somewhere overhead.

The footage ended abruptly. The woman reporter was back on the television. She had one hand flat against the side of her face, her finger pressed to an earpiece. Behind her another ambulance raced towards the hospital's emergency entrance.

The camera zoomed past the announcer's shoulder and focused on the ambulance as the driver leaped urgently from the vehicle and ran to the back doors. He flung them open. Then, suddenly, a blood-covered woman leaped from inside the vehicle. She was young and slim, her face and hair red with gore. She was wearing a blouse and skirt. The blouse had been ripped open. She attacked the ambulance man with an enraged roar, clawing at his eyes. Her weight drove him backwards and he crashed to the ground, flailing his arms and screaming in terror. The woman snarled at him and her eyes were wild and inhuman. She tore at the man's face, ripping flesh from around his mouth and then gouged at his eyes. The man thrashed and kicked. The woman trapped one of his arms and gnawed the ambulance man's wrist. The guy screamed – a blood-curdling roar of pain and terror, and clutched at the mangled wound.

The woman was hunched on his chest like a beast driven to maddened frenzy. She lunged at the ambulance driver's neck and ripped at the flesh, then slowly lifted her head and looked around her. Her gaze was distant and mindless but when she saw the camera man and reporter, she became instantly alert.

The woman reporter screamed.

The ghoul spat the ambulance man's flesh from its mouth and rose slowly to its feet. She was awash with fresh blood. It dripped from her hands and from her face. It clotted on her blouse and down her legs. She opened her mouth and moaned.

The camera pulled back until the woman reporter was in focus. She had her back turned, still staring at the bloody nightmare by the open doors of the ambulance. Slowly she turned back to face the camera. Her face was bloodless white with shock. She was crying pitifully.

"Oh, God," the reporter sobbed softly. "Oh, my God." She dropped to her knees, as though all the strength had suddenly gone from her body.

In the background the ghoul began to stagger towards the camera.

Arthur Harrigan heaved himself out of the recliner and went to the bedroom. He had a pistol in the bedside drawer – an old revolver. He loaded the weapon with fumbling, trembling fingers and tucked it inside the belt of his trousers.

Somewhere outside – maybe on the next block – he heard a gun shot. Then another. He froze for a moment. Far away – the sound ebbing and fading on the breeze – was the familiar wail of a police siren. Arthur went to the bedroom window and ripped the curtains open.

The afternoon was bright and sunny, but there was a haze of dark smoke on the horizon, billowing black and rising up like an ugly scar into the blue sky.

Arthur went back into the living room. He stood by the window and checked the driveway. The street seemed clear – almost eerily quiet.

The sirens in the distance were getting louder, coming closer. He took the gun from his belt. Somehow the comforting weight of the weapon in his hand made him feel better.

Safer.

He locked the front door. Then went through the hallway into the kitchen to secure the back door. When he came back into the living room, there was a grim-faced man on the television. He looked to be in his fifties. He had thinning grey hair. His eyes were dark and somber under bushy eyebrows. He was wearing a white lab coat, and sitting stiffly behind a table covered in a twisting nest of microphones and voice recorders. Behind the man was a blue curtain, with an embroidered white motif and the words 'Centers for Disease Control' beneath it. A thin red graphic at the bottom of the television screen flashed 'Live from Atlanta'.

Arthur edged closer to the television.

" – *morning about one hundred cases had been reported,"* a journalist's voice off camera was saying. *"Is there an update on the number of people who have now been infected?"*

The spokesman stared stonily at the camera. *"Over a thousand,"* he said, *"and still counting."*

There was a murmur of voices, a flash of cameras, and then suddenly people seemed to be shouting at once. A single voice rose above the others.

"Do you know how the outbreak started... or where it originated from?"

The spokesman shook his head heavily. *"No,"* he admitted. *"The first suspicious report from Baltimore was of an Egyptian merchant seaman who was taken to Baltimore General late Tuesday afternoon. It remains unconfirmed whether that man was patient zero."*

"Unconfirmed?" one of the journalists sounded incredulous. *"Why? Are you still running tests?"*

"No," the spokesman said. *"We... the hospital cannot locate the body."*

A stunned pall fell over the room. The CDC spokesman blinked under the harsh lights and mopped sweat from his brow. The man's hand was trembling.

"Does the C.D.C have the outbreak under control?" a new voice asked.

"No." the spokesman said frankly.

Another clamor of voices, rising louder, desperate to be heard.

"Do you know what we're dealing with?"

"No," the man said. *"But it appears to be viral. An infection that is being spread through bites and bodily fluid contamination. It's unlike anything we have ever encountered before."*

"Is it true these infected people are... are coming back to life after being killed?"

The man said nothing.

"What areas are being affected? How widespread is the outbreak?" another reported asked in the brief silence.

The spokesman turned his head and looked directly towards the reporter who had asked the question. *"Baltimore... but spreading quickly,"* the man said. *"We've already had reports from as far away as Virginia in the south and Pennsylvania to the north."*

The voices of the reporters became riotous, rising in a roar of disbelief. A woman's voice, sounding almost hysterical, shouted above the noise.

"What do we do? What can be done to stop the spread?"

Before the spokesman could answer, a second voice cried out, *"Is this a plague?"*

"There is nothing we can do," the CDC spokesman said flatly in response to the first question. Then he paused for a long moment as though gathering his thoughts. When he spoke, his words were measured and deliberate. *"At this stage we are advising people to stay in their houses and avoid contact with anyone. Anyone,"* he said again to emphasize the point. *"Infection spreads through bite attacks. You should do all you can to ensure you remain isolated from anyone displaying symptoms of erratic behavior, or people with a clear disposition of anger or violence. Stay in your house ... and pray."*

There was another burst of camera flashes, and then a young man entered the picture. He clutched at the spokesman's arm and bent close to his ear to whisper urgently. The spokesman listened. Then he looked up suddenly and sharply into the young man's face. The other man nodded. The CDC spokesman screwed his eyes tightly shut for a long moment while the world watched on in silence. Finally, the man turned back towards the camera. His eyes were wet with tears and his face stricken with pure fear.

"In the time I have been speaking to you, another thousand cases have been reported to medical staff

16

across the north east of the country," the spokesman said. *"Officially... the virus is out of control."*

The room fell into shocked silence. Finally one reporter asked almost fearfully. *"What... what are you calling the outbreak? Does it have a name?"*

The spokesman shook his head. *"The infection is uncategorized,"* he said.

"Is this a zombie virus?" one reported asked, and his tone was earnest and fearful.

"Yes," the spokesman said after a long agonizing pause, *"because quite frankly I don't know any other terminology to explain it. The infected are bitten and die in agony. Then they rise again. There is only one other word for it."*

"Which is?"

"Armageddon," the spokesman answered. *"This is the end of days. The end of life in America as we know it."*

Arthur Harrigan stared at the television in disbelief. He felt cold. A superstitious dread crawled like ice through his veins until his body trembled uncontrollably. He snatched for the phone. Suddenly he wanted more than anything else to hear the voice of his daughter.

He called the number and stood in the hallway listening to the hollow tone as it rang out. He dialed again – then suddenly the front door exploded back against its hinges, and a blood-covered nightmare of horror burst into the house.

Arthur cried out in shock and terror. The phone fell from his hands.

It was a man. His left arm had been torn from his body, his clothes just dirty ragged shreds that hung from his broken shape in tatters. It groaned – a low vicious sound of rage in the back of its throat. It saw

Arthur and its sunken yellowed eyes flashed. It snarled.

Arthur Harrigan snatched up the pistol and fired once, hitting the ghoul in the chest. The beast reeled backwards. It crashed against the hallway wall and smeared long streaks of fresh dripping blood on the wallpaper. Then it regained its balance, seemingly driven to frenzy by the roar of the weapon's blast. It snarled at Arthur and lunged for him, its fingers seized into blood-dripping vicious claws.

Arthur jammed the pistol hard against his own temple. His last thought was of his wife. Then he pulled the trigger.

* * *

Tammy Scott died because she was young and reckless.

There was a place down by the river near her childhood home that Tammy would hide when her father came home drunk and her parents began to fight.

It was a quiet place; somewhere she could retreat to when life seemed dark and uncertain.

She wished she could go there now.

She wished for that more than anything else. Because if she were there – in her quiet happy place – she wouldn't be staring at herself in the mirror and contemplating the dreadful thing she was about to do.

"Haven't you got higher heels?"

"No."

Margie dropped onto the narrow bed and looked at her friend. "Turn around."

Tammy turned awkwardly, feeling acutely embarrassed.

"Mess your hair up. It looks too tidy."

Obediently Tammy scraped her fingers through her blonde hair, letting it tumble over her shoulders.

"Is that denim skirt the shortest one you've got?" Margie ran her eyes up to the tops of her friend's smooth brown thighs.

Tammy frowned. "Jesus, Margie. How much shorter can a skirt be? Anything with less material is called a belt!"

Margie pulled a face. She stood up. "You've gotta give a glimpse of the merchandise," she said. She unfastened three of the buttons on Tammy's white blouse, revealing the lacy tops of her red bra. "Competition is tough. You've got really nice tits. You ought to show 'em off."

Tammy took a deep breath and wished that she could stop her legs from trembling. She stood still while Margie pulled the collar of her blouse off her shoulder a little, pushed and prodded at her hair, and then painted her lips with bright red lipstick. "You'll do," Margie sighed. "But don't overprice yourself. You're not eighteen. You're twenty-two. That means you're old in this game."

Tammy nodded. In the background, she could hear some kind of an urgent news bulletin on the radio. She tried to focus on the sound of the reporter's voice, but Margie was still talking. Tammy frowned, somehow suddenly uneasy. She leaned across to turn the volume up, but Margie slapped at her hand to get her attention.

"And try to pretend tonight that you're not a wide eyed innocent waitress from Cornpoke Arizona," Margie insisted. "The reason you haven't had a single date your first two nights on the street is because your scaring the business away. No guy wants to put his money down for a good time with the girl next door. They're looking for Lara Croft."

Tammy turned her head sharply.

"What?"

"Girl, they're looking for some action! When I worked the streets I done real good because I was nasty – full of attitude and up for anything. That's what you've gotta do if you wanna actually make some money."

Jesus! Tammy cringed.

"Most guys cruising for sex are looking for a sixteen year old girl who looks like she's twelve," Margie explained. "You can't compete with that, so you gotta offer something different. You gotta be the experienced confident score."

"How can I possibly do that?" Tammy fretted. "Margie, I've only had one boyfriend – and that was three years ago. I can't do experienced. I can't –"

"Just wiggle your ass and walk like you own it," Margie said. "And be confident. When a car pulls up at the curb, you saunter over, lean in the window so they can get a good look down your top, and ask in a real sexy voice if they want to party. It's easy."

"Easy for you, maybe."

Margie rolled her eyes. "Honey, the rule in this game is that you gotta fake it until you make it."

Tammy's hands were bunched into anxious fists. She took one last look at herself in the mirror and cringed. She threw her handbag over her shoulder and tried to keep her balance on the threadbare carpet.

"I don't want to make it," Tammy said. "I am just doing this to make ends meet."

"Make it... make ends meet... its all the same thing, honey. That's why Angelo is going to meet you in the alley," Margie said. "Tonight he'll take you to your corner and keep watch."

"I told you I don't want anything to do with Angelo!" Tammy hissed. "This isn't a career, Margie. It's... it's just for a few nights until I can replace the rent money. I don't want to be one of Angelo's working girls."

"You ain't got a choice," Margie said. "You struck out two nights in a row on your own. Angelo has connections. It's worth the cut he takes."

"He's a pimp, you mean."

"He's protection," Margie insisted.

Tammy sighed. It was probably Angelo who had smashed her apartment window and robbed her, for all she knew. "Fine. I'll meet him in the alley. Then I'll decide."

Margie made another face. "Just don't piss him off," she said. "I know what you can be like. This is business. So keep your thoughts to yourself. It don't matter if you don't like him. It only matters that he protects you and makes sure you get paid. Remember, whatever you do – don't get him angry."

"Your boyfriend is an asshole," Tammy said.

"Be that as it may," Margie said primly, "but he's *my* asshole, and he's *your* bodyguard. We both need him."

Tammy bit her lip. She looked around her tiny apartment bedroom one last time and then picked up her keys from the bedside table.

"Will you still be here when I get back?"

"Where else would I go?" Margie asked.

Tammy kissed Margie on the cheek and tottered through the door, down the dark rickety staircase and out through the building's side exit.

The alley was narrow, walled on either side by dilapidated high-rise apartment blocks. Tammy glanced up through the crisscross maze of rusting fire escapes and curtained windows to the night sky. There were no stars. The night was black and she could smell smoke in the air.

The alley wasn't dark. City lights filled the narrow backstreet with a flickering glow as traffic snaked past garish neon signs. Tammy stepped past piled plastic bags of trash and wheeled dumpsters filled to overflowing.

There was a huddle of dark shapes in the alley, their bodies silhouetted. Tammy tugged self-consciously at the hem of her denim skirt and walked towards them. Her heels echoed loudly on the ground and the group of figures changed shape as they turned toward the sound. Then one man broke away from the others and swaggered towards Tammy.

"Well now," the man's face appeared from the shadows as he neared. "Don't you look fine."

Tammy stood still and sighed. "Hi Angelo."

He was a tall broad-shouldered man with Latino features and a hawk-like nose. His long dark hair was pulled back behind his head in a greasy ponytail. He wore a white t-shirt and dirty jeans. He gazed at Tammy with piercing dark eyes and rubbed his chin as he circled her.

"You've certainly got it going there, girl," he smiled wolfishly. "You certainly do."

Tammy folded her arms and stared at Angelo listlessly. "Are you finished?"

He laughed. "Well actually... I'm only just starting. You see, I gotta taste the goods before I put 'em on sale, Lilly. So how about you and I go somewhere more comfortable, and you can show me what you're offering?"

"No chance," Tammy sneered. "And I don't think Margie would like to hear what you just said either."

Angelo pointed his finger. "Girl, I am serious," he said suddenly. "None of my bitches goes on the street until I get to sample her wares. That's the way it was for Margie when she worked, and it's the way it is for every other bitch I protect. You ain't special."

He closed the space between them, his expression dark, his eyes menacing. Tammy took an uncertain step backwards. She heard a police siren wailing somewhere close by, and the night seemed alive with frenetic noise and bustle. She blocked it all out and focused on the menace in front of her.

Angelo's raised voice had drawn the attention of the two other men. They started down the alleyway.

"Bro? You got trouble?"

"This little bitch ain't a good sharer," he called over his shoulder. "It's nothin'."

The two men exchanged sniggers of laughter and turned away. Tammy watched them retreat into the shadows. When she flicked her eyes back to Angelo, there was a leering smile on his face, and a short-bladed knife held low in one of his hands.

"What the –?"

"I ain't got time to play with you, girl," Angelo said. "Every minute you're standin' here and not on your back is costing me money. Now my boys think you're giving me lip. That ain't good for my business. Now I know you got a mouth on you. I want to see it go to work." With his free hand Angelo began to tug at the zipper on his jeans. "And if you ever tell Margie I got a free sample, I'll come back with this knife and cut out your tongue. Business is business. You wanna be on the game, you gotta play by my rules."

Tammy's eyes widened. She took another step away, and felt cold damp bricks against her back. Angelo saw the startled expression in her eyes.

"Nowhere else to go," he said softly. "So it's time to get down and party. Only now, we don't do it comfortable – we do it nasty. I'm just gonna throw you down on some trash bags and do you. 'Cause... that's what you are now, right? White trash."

Tammy couldn't take her eyes off the glinting silver blade. In Angelo's hand it weaved slowly from side to side like the hypnotic dance of a deadly snake. The taste of her fear was thick in her throat. She could feel her heart racing, pounding hard against the cage of her ribs.

Angelo drifted closer. It was just one more step, but he was so close now he was within striking distance. Tammy heard him growl at her and she glanced up at his face. His teeth were bared in a malicious snarl.

Tammy slowly eased the strap of her handbag of her shoulder and held up her hands in resignation. "Alright," she whispered. "Alright..." Her handbag splashed into a muddy puddle. She brought one of her hands down to the front clasp of her bra, and as Angelo leered at her, she suddenly lashed out with a vicious kick.

Tammy's heel socked into Angelo's crotch with a meaty thump. All her anger and fear was behind the blow and she felt the instant satisfaction as it landed heavily between his legs.

For a moment Angelo froze, and then he slowly toppled sideways like a felled tree, his hands clutching low at his stomach, his face twisted into a rictus of agony.

Tammy turned and ran.

The darkened alley was a dead-end. Tammy knew her only chance of escape was to get past Angelo's two minders. It was the only way out of the alley. She started to run, screaming as loudly as she could.

"Help!" she shouted at the two dark shapes. She waved her arms and then doubled over. The men ran towards her and when she stood up again she had her heels in her hands.

"It's Angelo!" she said breathlessly, her eyes wide. "I think he's been shot."

The two men looked at each other, their expressions stunned. On the ground, deeper into darkened alley, they could see Angelo writhing on the pavement.

Tammy raced past the men. As she got nearer to the corner, the light from the city and the noise of passing traffic grew louder and more chaotic. A police car flashed past at high speed, and then she heard a woman's chilling scream and a screech of brakes.

Tammy ran out of the alley and turned left without thinking.

Then froze.

The world was on fire. The Laundromat and a Chinese restaurant on the corner were ablaze and there were scattered groups of terrified people running in all directions. Some were carrying suitcases. Others were carrying guns. Their faces were ghastly white and filled with manic horror. She saw one man swing a baseball bat at a car's window, but the sound of the glass shattering was drowned out by the panicked screams of three women who were running straight towards her. Tammy's stared in confusion and sudden panic. The frantic fear on the women's faces, and the chilling sound of their shrieks above the clamor of wailing sirens and alarms was infectious. She felt herself overcome by an ominous sense of dread.

Then, from a dark alley across the road, Tammy saw two blood-drenched figures emerge onto the sidewalk. They were big, bulky shapes, moving briskly towards her, lit by the bright orange glow of the burning buildings. Tammy screamed. A surge of panic filled her. One of the figures was naked. Tammy could see the man's chest had been torn open. Its entrails hung in long twisted slimy ropes as it moved, and its face was a mask of dripping blood. It hissed at Tammy, and there was an enraged murderous frenzy in its eyes.

She turned to run, but suddenly a figure crashed through the glass front of the Chinese restaurant. It was a man – and he was on fire. He lumbered across the sidewalk and onto the street, twisting and turning and squealing in a blazing pyre, like a human torch, until it seemed he could go no further and finally collapsed to his knees in the middle of the road.

Horns blared. Tyres screeched. And then a dark colored SUV came hurtling past at high speed and crashed the burning man to the ground. Tammy screamed again. Headlights blinded her, and panicked voices shouted violent abuse. She turned to flee, jinking past a middle-aged man who was carrying a television set in his arms, then stepped out onto the road.

And lost her footing.

Tammy staggered – whirled round in terror – and fell directly into the path of a swerving, speeding car.

* * *

Jack Cutter survived because a wall fell on him.

He was running – running for his life – sweat staining the front of his t-shirt, his breathing labored. All around him the world was going to hell.

And he didn't know why.

It had happened within a matter of moments. One minute he was parking his pick-up and walking towards the center of town under a clear blue sky – and the next he was struggling to stay alive as the street filled with hordes of screaming, terrified people, and the air overhead thumped with the heavy vibrating beat of helicopter rotors.

The windows of a department store exploded outwards in a fireball of searing hot flame and deadly shards of glass. The shock of the blast was so fierce that the ground around him trembled and the sidewalk seemed to heave beneath his feet. A woman in front of him tripped and fell, and Cutter stumbled over her. The concrete smeared skin from his hands, and for a stunned moment he could only lay still, covering his face from the scattering feet and legs all around him. The noise was deafening; the panic-stricken screams of office workers, and mothers who clutched desperately at their children – all overlaid by the constant thump of the helicopters and the plaintive wail of car horns as horrified motorists abandoned their vehicles and fled the madness on foot.

Cutter heard a sporadic volley of ragged gunfire from somewhere close behind, and the sound was enough to galvanize him. He struggled to his feet, bumped and jostled by the mindless horde.

The scene was chaotic. Thick smoke was billowing from the upper stories of the burning department store, and he could see a woman in a white blouse at a third floor window. She was screaming, flailing her arms in a desperate plea for help. Then she just disappeared – violently jerked out of sight by a strong clutching arm.

Overhead, two army helicopters were circling the madness, tilting in a series of sharp turns, and weaving above the city's rooftops. Cutter heard a ragged burst of machine gun fire and saw the winking red flashes of light – and stood frozen and appalled as he realized the choppers were firing into the confusion.

He turned and ran. The sound of the crowd's panic undulated like a wave of noise, rising and falling like a heart-gripping herald of doom. Gunfire ripped through the air indiscriminately, stitching ragged fragments from the blacktop, and sawing though cars and people. The street billowed in fresh pyres of smoke and flame, and the crowd's panic turned to hysteria.

A four-wheel-drive suddenly broke from the jammed line of abandoned cars, shunting and crumpling its way up onto the sidewalk and scything a path through the teeming crowds. The desperate scattered, but those who were too slow to react were tossed over the hood like pieces of broken debris, or dragged under the savage tread of the huge terrain tires. The motor roared as the vehicle veered in wild arcs, crashing into benches and trash cans.

Cutter heard the howl of the revving engine and turned just in time. He saw the wild, wide eyes of the driver behind the windshield. Saw the man's mouth open in a roar of frantic panic – and threw himself sideways. He felt the fender of the truck smash his foot a glancing blow, and then he crashed into a doorway as the big roaring vehicle careered over the woman who had fallen in front of Cutter, crushing and killing her instantly.

The vehicle rocked wildly on its suspension. The left side wheels became airborne and the right side wheels dug into the gutter in a wicked howl of smoke and rubber. The vehicle teetered sideways, its momentum carrying it into the front of a burger shop on the corner of the block. The collision stopped the vehicle dead, and the driver was hurled through the windshield head-first by the shocking impact. He was torn to pieces by the falling, shattering glass of the shop front, and his body impaled to the hood of his vehicle.

The awning over the front of the building collapsed in a scream of rending metal and crumbling bricks. Cutter tucked himself into a ball and covered his head with his hands. Thick dust and debris enveloped him as the front of the building slowly began to fall and the noise around him sounded loud as the end of the world.

For long moments of eerie, stunned silence, Cutter lay perfectly still. When he finally opened his eyes his world was a small tight space of rubble and billowing dust. He coughed, spat gritty dirt from his mouth, and dragged his hands across his face and eyes. He saw jagged shapes of daylight, and he kicked out at the debris that pinned his legs.

Slowly he turned his head sideways. There was a dead man lying close beside him, his body cleaved in half by a ragged piece of iron. A warm pool of blood was leaking across the sidewalk, congealing into a brown kind of mud. Beside the carnage was the shape of another man in a white shirt and trousers who had his back to him. Cutter rolled onto his side and reached out with his fingers. The man flinched, and then raised a feeble hand to his face.

Cutter sat up. Iron girders and broken masonry lay in fractured, twisted chaos all around him. He got to his knees, then hunched over and coughed again. He could see the side of the four-wheel-drive. The roof of the vehicle had been crushed flat under the weight of the awning. He could see the driver's legs hanging limp across the hood, but nothing more.

The man in the white shirt rolled onto his back and groaned. His face was a mask of grey dust, and there was a bleeding gash on his cheek. His shirt was covered in dirt and spattered blood, but he was breathing. Cutter crawled over the dead body and shook the man's shoulders.

"You all right?" Cutter croaked.

The man groaned again.

Cutter crouched over the man and pushed away a piece of iron sheeting. Through the space he could see the city street.

Buildings were on fire. The air was thick with billowing clouds of black smoke, but overhead the army helicopters still circled vengefully, dipping low in strafing runs like prehistoric predators, their powerful rotors ripping through the haze as the machine guns continued to fire.

Wrecked, mangled cars choked the street. Alarms sounded piercing and plaintive. People cried out in fear and pain. And on the sidewalk, not twenty feet away, Cutter noticed a woman in a grey business suit, hunched over the body of a young girl wearing a bright summer dress. The woman was drenched in blood, and for an instant Cutter thought she was trying to rouse the child and rescue it. Then he saw the woman's head coil back, pause – and lunge at the child's neck to gorge on the girl's flesh. Cutter's eyes went wide with horror and shock. He heard the woman snarl as she tore at the child's body, and when the woman looked up again, her chin was dripping with blood that spilled all the way down her throat and soaked her blouse.

The child was still alive. Cutter saw the girl's thin brown legs thrashing. He watched on, numb with horror. Then the woman's snapping jaws gouged a vicious snarling bite from the girl's face and after another moment the child moved no more.

Cutter felt his stomach heave and tasted thick oily bile in the back of his throat. He bunched his fists, filled with black unholy rage that defied reason. He cried out, shouting through cracked lips at the woman, and grabbed for a piece of twisted iron pipe that had fallen when the awning had collapsed.

He took a staggering step towards the woman, and then suddenly felt a hand on his ankle, the grip fierce and desperate.

"Don't!" the man lying on the ground beside him gasped. "She's one of the infected."

Cutter stared down at the man, incredulous. "Infected?"

"The zombie virus," the man said, his voice a dry rasp. "It's been on the news. The whole of Virginia is being over-run."

Cutter shook his head, bewildered. He lowered the iron bar and felt a creeping icy numbness begin to spread through his body. He shook his head again, looked back at the woman – and then beyond her.

He could see other figures moving amongst the streaming mass of humanity. Blood-drenched shapes moved slowly – shuffling in the throng, clawing randomly. He saw one of the figures clutch at a running woman's shoulder and pull her off balance. The woman was young – maybe in her twenties. She fell on her back, hitting the ground hard, and was suddenly set upon by two more shambling shapes that seemed instinctively to sense her. The woman had a pistol in her hand. She screamed in fear and fired three quick rounds, point-blank into one figure's chest, flinging it back against the side of a car. But by then the other ghoul was tearing the young woman's guts wide open. Cutter heard her scream once more – a loud blood-chilling cry of agony and terror – and then more running people swept past and he lost sight of the woman in the chaos.

Cutter turned his attention back to the man lying at his feet within the debris of the wrecked building. The guy was groaning painfully, clutching at his chest, and despite the superficial cut to his face, Cutter was pretty sure the man had suffered internal injuries. The guy spat bright red blood onto the sidewalk and wiped the back of his hand across his mouth. He was shaking – maybe going into shock.

"Help me," the man pleaded. He was trying to claw himself upright. Cutter heaved him up, and felt his weight heavy against him as the man swayed on a damaged ankle.

"Broken?"

The guy shook his head. "I don't think so," he said, then winced and looked around, as if to get his bearings. He pointed past Cutter's shoulder. "The bookshop," he said. "That's where I work. There is a basement. We need to hide."

Cutter followed the direction of the man's arm. Across the street he could see the shop front for 'Newbridge City Books'. He shook his head. It was an old two-story building that had been built before the Second World War, with delicate ornate masonry around the upper floor windows and a wide display area on the ground floor beside a dark opening.

"We'll never make it," Cutter said. "Not in this madness."

The guy sagged heavily. His arm was draped over Cutter's shoulder. "We have to."

Cutter stared at the guy. He was in his early thirties, a thin, wiry shape with short hair and a long sallow face that was screwed up in the agony of his pain. But his eyes were clear and determined.

Cutter nodded. "Okay," he said.

In the first few moments of madness, the crowd on the streets had moved like a tide of humanity, spilling onto the roads and sidewalks and moving like a mass in one direction that had swept Jack Cutter up and carried him away. But now the crowds had lost their cohesion and direction, so that to Cutter it now seemed like the street had degenerated into an urban warfare battleground.

Pitched battles and running skirmishes were being fought as infected zombies clutched and dragged at the fleeing throng, and the victims turned and struggled with frenzied desperation for their lives. The screaming became louder, more piercing. The sounds of sporadic gunfire cracked and echoed between the tall buildings. Police sirens wailed in the distance, but never seemed to come closer – and through it all the remorseless clatter of the helicopters overhead tore at the air.

Cutter kicked aside more fallen bricks and his boots crunched on broken glass until he was standing on the edge of the sidewalk. The infected woman who was hunched over the body of the dead girl glanced up at Cutter, sensing his movement. Cutter watched the woman and felt a tremor of superstitious dread.

For long moments the undead woman watched him, her mouth open, and there was a dry retching sound in the back of her throat. Then she got to her feet and hissed.

Cutter moved slowly. He picked up the iron bar in his free hand and hefted the reassuring weight of it. It was about three feet long, some kind of iron pipe that might have been part of a drainage or plumping system before the burger shop had collapsed. It was crushed and bent at one end into a crude jagged hook.

With the man leaning heavily against him, Cutter stepped out onto the blacktop.

The undead woman snarled. She kicked the young girl aside, and Cutter thought he saw the body twitch. Then all his attention went back to the blood-soaked woman as she started to shamble towards him.

She was moving quickly, her gait awkward, like each step was a convulsion. Her body seemed to writhe and thrash. One of her legs dragged heavily, but her arms reached out, and her fingers seized into claws. Cutter watched in horror.

On his own, he could easily outrun the woman. But weighed down by the injured guy, he knew there was little hope of escape. Cutter got as far as the middle of the traffic-choked street, and accepted they weren't going to make it.

He leaned the guy against the bullet-riddled hood of a small silver sedan. Through the shattered windshield, Cutter could see the body of a woman driver. She was slumped back in her seat, her face torn away, the skull shattered. Blood and gore had sprayed across the interior so it looked like some kind of abstract artist's nightmare.

"Wait here," Cutter said. "And keep an eye out for others."

He turned back.

The undead woman was coming closer, remorseless and relentless. No caution, no sense of awareness – just a mindless instinct to hunt and kill driving its steps and blazing in it's yellowed jaundiced eyes. Cutter swung the pipe like a baseball bat and felt the solid sock of the weapon as it staved in the woman's unprotected ribs. The impact jarred all the way up his arms, and the woman was flung sideways like a rag doll, sent crashing against the trunk of a Buick. Cutter swung again, this time with more momentum, and with his legs well balanced. The iron pipe hissed through the air and the jagged hook of the weapon buried itself deep into the woman's back. It wailed in fury. It's head turned on its shoulders and it's eyes flashed with maddened rage. Cutter felt the icy chill of dread reach all the way to his heart and squeeze tight.

He tugged at the pipe, but it was buried deeply into bone and muscle. He twisted it, and the undead woman turned and lashed out at him with fingers clawed like bloody talons. Cutter swayed out of reach and kicked out at the woman's blood-spattered legs. She fell to the ground and the jagged hook of the pipe tore free. Cutter moved quickly. He stamped his foot into the middle of the woman's back. The zombie flailed its legs and scrabbled at the ground with its hands. Cutter swung the pipe down hard, swinging it like an axe, and burying the hook into the undead woman's skull.

She went still. Didn't move again. Cutter stood over the body for long seconds, breathing hard. He was shaking. His hands were trembling like a man in fever. Then he felt a hand seize his arm and he swung around wild with rage and fear.

It was the guy. He was pointing across the street. "More of them," he said.

In the building beside the book shop, a woman was standing at second floor window. She was screaming hysterically. She had a baby clutched in her arms, holding the bundle of blankets close to her chest, while behind her a blood-covered figure was clawing and tearing at her body with its teeth. The woman shrieked and slowly collapsed. The baby fell from her grip, out through the window. It hit the ground with the sickening thud of breaking, crushing bones.

Cutter turned away. He closed his eyes for just a moment and let the crazed madness of sirens and fire and screams and death wash over him like the shock wave after an explosion. He swayed, felt the world tilting at an impossible angle – but when he opened his eyes again he felt an instinctive surge of resolve and the need to survive. He hoisted the man's arm over his shoulder and dragged his limping weight on towards the book store.

Suddenly a roar of semi-automatic gunfire tore through the screams and chaos, and Cutter looked up in shock.

There was a man by the entrance of the store, barricaded in the open doorway behind an upturned desk. He was a big guy, with huge muscled shoulders, wearing a t-shirt with the sleeves torn off. Cutter saw the man wave at him urgently. The man was shouting something but the roar of more gunfire drowned the sound out. Cutter saw a bright red muzzle flash of light, and then felt the hiss of air as bullets flew close past him. He crouched instinctively, dragged like an anchor by the weight of the man at his side, and then fell to his knees. The man slipped from his arm and rolled painfully to the ground.

"Leave him!" the guy in the book shop entrance was shouting.

Cutter glanced over his shoulder. Undead figures were swarming towards him. They had been men and women, but now they were a walking nightmare of horribly disfigured, torn shapes, each moving stiffly and slowly, snapping their jaws and reaching out with clawed fingers towards him.

Cutter grabbed frantically at the guy's arm and tried to heave himself upright. The guy was like a leaden weight.

The book store was just fifteen feet away.

Cutter knew they weren't going to make it.

The undead shambled closer. One lunged for him but Cutter kicked out and drove the figure staggering backwards. Then he grabbed the injured guy's arm and tried to drag him to his feet.

More gunfire ripped around his head. He saw one of the zombies flung to the ground in a spatter of thick brown congealed ooze, and he heaved desperately at the injured man until he was upright and they were ten feet away from the store's open doorway.

The guy behind the barricade rose to his feet, standing like a colossus in the doorway. He was a man-mountain. He had a dark sunburned face, rugged features and a jaw like an anvil. He had long black hair down to his shoulders, but it was tied back by a scrap of material like a bandanna. There was a black nylon bag slung over his arm and some kind of a machine gun, tucked tight in against his shoulder. The weapon was aimed directly at Jack Cutter.

"Down!"

Cutter reached the curb. He heard the man shout, and he crashed to the concrete instinctively. Gunfire roared in a long ragged pulse of deafening noise. Empty shell casings spewed from the breach of the weapon in a heated arc – and then Cutter was dragging himself wearily back to his feet. He didn't look around. He didn't dare. He grabbed the injured guy's arm and clenched his teeth with the last of his strength and the final reserves of his will and determination.

Cutter heard a loud undulating moan close behind him. It was a sound that seemed demented and inhuman. He wrenched the injured guy to his feet – and made one last futile lunge to reach the bookstore.

The guy on his shoulder was dead weight. His legs were barely moving. Cutter could feel the limp heaviness of him dragging him down like an anchor. The man groaned. His breathing was shallow, coming in fractured uncertain ragged gasps, and his skin was burning hot to the touch.

Cutter heaved him bodily up onto the sidewalk. He could feel his knees going. He could feel the tremendous burden drain the last final reserves of his strength. He sensed the undead gathering close behind him. The sound of moaning was like the siren of his impending death. He took another step, then another...

And then there was the crack of a single shot, so loud it was shattering – and so close that he sensed the track of the bullet and heard the loud meaty slap as it crashed into its target. The man he was carrying slipped slowly from his grasp and fell dead to the sidewalk.

Cutter looked up in alarm. The big guy standing in the doorway was slowly lowering his weapon; smoke still curling in grey tendrils from the barrel. The two men locked eyes for a single second, and then the big man was heaving at the desk and clearing a breach in the barricade.

Cutter felt suddenly weightless; like he was hovering an inch above the ground. He went through the door at a run, tripping over debris so that he fell in an awkward tumble onto soft thick carpeting.

Jack Cutter was a big man himself; six-two, and still in good shape for a thirty-three year old guy who had played a little college ball before discovering he had a talent for art. But the gunman was a monster. He heaved Cutter to his feet effortlessly and dragged him towards the back of the book shop.

There were two women standing, fearful and crying and waiting, by shelves of fantasy novels. They were clinging to each other, both trembling, their expressions dazed with shock. The big guy nodded at the women as he swept past.

"There's no more to save," he said. "It's time to get to the shelter."

The group ran past high timber stands of paperback novels and children's books, then past an ancient elevator. Cutter followed the broad shape of the gunman's back as he carved a path towards the darkened rear of the building.

They heard a clamor of noise behind them: the sound of glass shattering and furniture being overturned. Something crashed to the ground with enough force to make the floor shudder. The woman next to Cutter screamed. Then the gunman was slamming his shoulder hard against the back wall of the building, beside a closed iron door.

It was a huge grey-metal slab of steel – some kind of a fire door. There was a sign that read 'Staff Only' in big red lettering, and underneath it was the word 'Escape'. The gunman hammered the butt of the machine gun against the steel three times and Cutter heard the sound echo.

An instant later the door opened cautiously outwards, and Cutter saw the pale terrified face of a blonde woman in the darkened recess beyond. She might have been pretty – but her eyes were tragic and huge, her face streaked and smeared with tears.

"There's no one else," the big guy said. "These three are the only ones I could save."

He put his hand in the middle of Cutter's back and shoved him through the opening, followed by the two women. Then he heaved the door closed behind him until it slammed in place and locked tight, shutting them away from the chaos of a world in ruin.

Two.
Apocalypse.

Cutter was standing on a narrow landing. He could see steps descending towards a corridor bright with fluorescent lighting. The walls were rough cold brick, covered with ancient concrete masonry. He followed the blonde woman down the stairs and realized the corridor opened into a vast basement area. But it wasn't just one large room; it was an area with darkened corners that had once been smaller rooms, and black narrow passageways. He glanced around, frowning. Off to his right he could see a wide opening and another room, maybe twenty feet square that was also bright with lighting.

The open area he stood in was cold and musty. The floor was concrete and the area was divided by high timber stands, each one filled with books of every description. To his left, set against the wall, was a long conveyor belt that led towards a solid timber door set into the far wall. Two men were standing by the doorway, holding hammers and breathing raggedly. They came towards Cutter and the others, their expressions bleak. This part of the basement was gloomy, the lighting not strong enough to penetrate every shadowed recess. The gunman brushed past Cutter and met the two men.

"Done?"

One of the men nodded. He was an older guy, maybe in his fifties. He was wearing a white business shirt, silk tie and grey trousers. He had the ruddy complexion of a man who was not used to physical labor. He was sweating.

"Boarded up," the business man said. "We used what we could find in the storeroom. I think it will hold."

The gunman looked a question at the other man holding a hammer. He was younger; a fresh faced kid who couldn't be more than twenty. He had an ugly red rash of acne scars on his cheeks and his eyes were red, as though he had been crying.

He nodded. "It will hold," he confirmed.

The gunman looked satisfied. He turned to Cutter and the other two women.

"This is your new home – at least temporarily," he said. Then he led them through the opening into the smaller, well-lit room. He set the rifle down on a corner bench and let the black nylon bag slip from his arm to the ground, while around him all of the survivors silently gathered.

The gunman turned and studied them carefully for long silent seconds. Cutter, and the two men holding hammers were the only other men in the room. Around them stood twelve women, including the two he had saved on the street. A couple of the women were in their fifties, the rest younger. He sighed.

"For those of you who don't know me, my name is Hos," he said. Then he stared at the guy in the business clothes. "Mr. Grainer, if it's all right with you, I'll be running things from now on."

The man nodded, and his expression was almost relieved. "Of course," he said.

Everyone apart from Cutter and the other rescued women knew each other. They were the book store's staff. Hos turned from the store manager until his eyes settled on the terrified faces of the women.

43

"There's no point sugar-coating what is happening at ground zero," Hos said, raising his voice so that his words carried clear and steady to everyone. "The fact is that our world has changed forever – and you better get used to it right now, because from what I've seen in the past twenty minutes, things are never going to be the same again."

There was an uneasy silence, and Hos let his words hang heavily in the air for a moment.

"Right now, the streets of Newbridge are being over-run by plague infected carriers. They're biting and killing everyone and everything they see. If you've been listening to the radio, this appears to be the same virus that has spread from Baltimore, and I don't think Newbridge is the only city affected," Hos swept his eyes across the shocked, pale faces. "In fact, I think the whole of Virginia – and maybe the whole of the eastern seaboard is being infected."

He paused again, giving time for the information to be absorbed. "These things don't just die," Hos said. "I shot a dozen of them – maybe more – and the only ones that didn't get up again were the ones who took hits to the head. Every other infected body I fired at got up again."

One of the women in the back of the group began to sob softly. Hos ignored her and pushed on.

"The army has helicopters overhead," he said, and he saw a look of sudden hope spread across the faces of the women standing closest. He crushed down on it brutally. "They're firing into the crowd," he said. "The army is firing at everything and everyone that moves. That means the Government has given up any hopes of containing the spread of the virus. That means they've abandoned any hope of rescuing people like us who are trapped here, still alive. It means the Government has declared Martial Law, and the army has orders to shoot to kill anything moving on the streets."

There were cries of anguish, and despairing moans. Several women were weeping, while others stared blankly as if seeing something beyond the walls of their refuge, their expressions grim.

Cutter felt a woman's shoulder slump against his. It was the blonde woman who had stood at the steel door and led them down into the basement. His arm went around her shoulder automatically, and he felt her shoulders heave as she began to sob.

Hos raised his hands to quieten everyone. He wasn't finished. "Crying isn't going to help," he said sternly. "It's not going to keep you alive. I've told you what I know, and what I've seen. The city and beyond is being destroyed and over-run by undead. They're relentlessly exterminating everyone still alive. And the Government has abandoned us. Accept it. Then we can start to deal with it."

"What are they?" Cutter asked Hos, and the big man turned to him.

"They're zombies. They're the undead."

Cutter almost laughed. Almost. But he could see the look in the big man's eyes. He wasn't joking. Then another voice in the crowd said softly, "that's what the media is calling them too," she confirmed. "It's some kind of a zombie virus that started in the Baltimore area. The CDC called them zombies."

"Then we're fucked," another woman said. She was a tall woman in a white blouse and grey skirt. She looked like she was in her early forties, but she had long grey hair and a deeply concerned frown of concentration on her face, as though somehow this problem was her responsibility to solve. She threw her hands in the air and trapped her lip between her teeth. "We're completely fucked!"

Other voices joined in the clamor, rising and becoming shrill and hysterical.

"We're not," Hos said, but his voice was drowned out by the soft panic wails of the group. He picked up the rifle and slammed the butt down on the bench top. "We're not!"

They turned to him then, shocked out of their own misery and black despair by the confidence and strength of his voice. It took another moment, but slowly the group settled. The sobbing became sniffles and they looked to him with desperation, as though he alone held the key to their survival.

"We're safe for the moment," Hos reassured the group. "And we have enough essentials to last a little while." The room they were gathered in had been set up as a staff lunch-room. There was a small microwave on a counter next to a sink, and a wooden table in the middle of the floor surrounded by four mis-matched worn chairs. Under a long timber bench top was a small refrigerator, and on top of the bench was an old television. "But we don't have a lot of food – certainly not enough to last us more than a day or two." he said. "But we are safe. This book shop used to be a bank," Hos explained. "This whole area was once the bank's vaults and storage areas. The shipping door at the back of the building has been secured – and there are no other ways in or out. But we need to prepare – quickly, so anyone who thinks they've got time for tears and misery can think again. Right now, we're all going to pull our weight. You can cry later."

"I can't stay here," a woman said from the back of the room, her voice outraged. She pushed herself forward, and her expression was filled with mindless terror. "I have children. They need me!" Her voice rose in panic. "I can't wait here for a day, or even an hour. I've got to get to my babies. I've got to get to my family!"

Hos cut the woman off, and his tone was harsh, almost brutal.

He took a long deep breath as though he were about to dive into deep water. "Stephanie, your family is most likely already dead," Hos said. "All our families are probably dead by now. The city is being over-run. Maybe the whole state and the country."

The woman sagged to her knees and began to tremble violently. Cutter heard her sobbing. One of the other women knelt beside her and wrapped a comforting arm around the woman's heaving shoulders.

"If anyone leaves this shelter, you'll be dead within minutes," Hos said brutally. "We have to assume that everyone we know has been bitten and infected. That means the families we had no longer exist. They're undead. You can't help them. You can't save them. It's already too late. All you can do is save yourself."

"Dammit, Hos! It's all right for you. You don't have a wife or kids. I have my husband and a small child to think about," another woman stood taller in the group and cried out in angry protest. Her voice was shrill. Other voices in the crowd began to swell in chorus, becoming heated and rising in panic. "What's the point of living if we've lost our families and loved ones?"

Hos stared them all down, cowering them to muttered resentful silence with the sheer force of his will. "I'm not talking about living, Suzie," he said grimly to one of the younger women. She was newly married and had just returned from her honeymoon a week before. She was working part-time. "I'm talking about surviving. That's all. Living comes later, and so do the regrets and the mourning. But right now we're fighting to survive."

Cutter stepped forward. "Hos is right," he said. "I saw what was happening up on the street. These zombie killers are infected with some kind of fury — some kind of mad rage. They're vicious and relentless. You can't kill them, which means you can't defend yourself. By now there are tens of thousand of them. I saw one girl bitten by a woman, and within minutes that young girl's body was twitching again, like her corpse was coming back to life. That means it can't be contained. And I saw the helicopters," he added grimly. "Hos is right. They're mowing down everyone — man woman and child. They're killing anything that moves. It's a slaughter."

Cutter saw heads begin to nod in meek, shocked understanding and some kind of remorseful guilt. One by one they turned slowly back towards the tall brooding shape of Hos.

The group had gravitated to this man, accepting him naturally as their leader, despite the store manager's authority. Cutter too was drawn to the sense of calm confidence the huge man seemed to radiate.

"What happens after a day or two of waiting, Hos?" John Grainger, the book store manager asked. His voice was shaky and filled with anguish. "Where will you lead us to?" His soft pink hands fluttered like bird's wings. "If the city and whole state has been over-run by zombies – where the hell can we go that will be safe, and what do we do?"

Hos shook his head slowly, and Cutter had the impression the big man was unwilling to answer the question directly. He felt a sudden sense of unease.

"It's too early to make that decision, Mr. Grainger," Hos said carefully. "It's going to depend on too many things that right now we don't have clear information about. But I expect the next day will be the worst. By then, anyone still alive in the city and surrounds will have fled to the countryside. There won't be anyone left alive, unless they managed to find the kind of shelter we have. So hopefully the undead will have drifted away from here, in search of others to infect. That's how the virus has spread so quickly. They seem to be driven to infect the living. They're not feasting on the bodies. What I saw on the street was a frenzy of slow-moving mindless killers that seemed hell-bent on biting to spread the contamination. They don't seem to be flesh-eaters, and that's a good thing. It means that once the initial terror has passed, there will be a lot less of them because they will be hunting further away to find new victims."

The young guy who Cutter had met in the warehouse was still holding a hammer, as though somehow it gave him a sense of security. "We need weapons, Hos," the kid said. "We need to find something we can fight these things with when we make our break."

Hos nodded. Apart from the AR-15 he was holding, he had two Glocks in the black nylon bug-out bag at his feet, as well as ammunition, a knife, flashlight, duct tape, rope, matches and other bare essentials.

"We'll make some weapons," Hos assured the kid. "But right now we have higher priorities."

He turned to the pretty blonde woman who had stood waiting at the steel door. "Glenda, I want you and a couple of the other women to start filling every container you can with water," Hos said, his voice was a gravel-like deep rumble. "We can't survive without plenty to drink."

The blonde nodded. Cutter noticed the woman's lip was trembling, like she was on the verge of tears, but somehow managing to hold it all together.

"Jennifer, you will monitor the television," Hos singled out an older woman who worked in the store. "I want to know what's happening, and where it's happening. I want to know what the army and police are doing. Understand?" The older woman nodded. She had a handkerchief in her hand, dabbing delicately at the corners of her eyes. "Sally, you and the rest of the women will be on your phones," Hos said. "We need to get the word out to everyone and anyone that we are here," he added, "and we need to do it quickly. There is no guarantee that the phone networks, or the power will last. I want you to call or message family and friends and every police station in Virginia. Tell them how many we are, and where we are located."

Sally was a tall, heavy-set brunette woman bulging out of a tight white blouse and a long blue skirt. She nodded, and snatched at her handbag. Then she turned to the rest of the women and gathered them around her like a mother hen counting her chicks.

Hos waited until the women were organized and occupied with their tasks. Then he took Cutter's arm and steered him away from the kitchen – back into the big gloomy storage room. John Grainer and the other young guy followed.

"We're going to wait it out down here for twenty-four hours," Hos explained to the men. "It's important we keep everyone busy – keep them distracted with tasks."

Cutter and the others around him nodded.

"We don't have enough food to last longer than that, and if we lose power in the meantime, these women are going to get hysterical in the dark," he added. "So we need to prepare a fire for light and warmth if that happens."

The young guy frowned. "We'll choke," he said. "Hos there's no ventilation down here. You said it yourself – this place is a vault. If we go lighting bonfires, the place will fill with smoke within an hour."

Hos nodded patiently. "I know, Jimmy," he said. "But we're not going to prepare bonfires. We're going to prepare old-fashioned torches. And they're only a precaution. I don't plan on lighting anything unless the power goes out."

The young guy nodded. The store manager stepped forward, tugging his tie loose and unfastening the top button of his shirt. "What do you want us to do?"

"Break apart a bookshelf, or find something we can wrap cloth around," Hos explained. "There are plenty of old cleaning rags in the store room. We just need something to wrap around them if the time comes."

John Grainger nodded. He grabbed the young man's elbow and steered him away towards one of the dark corridors Cutter had noticed earlier. Cutter watched the two men go. When he turned back, Hos was staring at him, like he was measuring his worth. The big man's eyes were narrowed and cunning. Cutter met and held his gaze defiantly.

Hos bristled. "You got something to say?"

"Yeah," Cutter nodded slowly, then stared the big man in the eyes. "I saw the way you shot," he said. "You're pretty handy with a gun."

The expression on Hos's face became a harsh mirthless smile. "It's a good gun," he said. "I call it Visa – because I never leave home without it."

Cutter grunted. "But you're also a murderer," he accused. "You killed that man I was helping in cold blood."

Hos said nothing for a long moment, and when he spoke his tone was dispassionate and remote, his voice lowered and masked by the rising sounds of bustling activity around them. "Yeah, I killed him," he admitted. "And maybe that does make me a murderer. But I also saved your fuckin' life – and what I did is no worse than what you did."

Cutter glared. "Meaning?"

"Meaning you were trying to commit suicide by trying to save the man," Hos stabbed his finger at Cutter. "So don't judge me."

The two men stared at each other for long moments, the tension between them rising.

"Why else would you do it?" Hos challenged Cutter. "You knew when you reached the middle of the road that you weren't going to make it dragging that guy with you. So why did you keep trying? Have you got some kind of a death wish?"

Cutter stared at Hos, his eyes black and cold. "I had my reasons."

Hos grunted. "Well your reasons left me with no choice but to put the guy down to save your ass. I wouldn't have had to shoot, if you hadn't been trying to kill yourself saving him."

There was another long moment of tension, and then Hos suddenly spread his arms wide in exasperation. "Take a look at where we are! Think about what is happening. The old rules no longer apply," Hos said. "Civilization went out the window when those undead mothers started infecting and killing people. I did what I had to do, and I'd do it again. I'm a survivalist," Hos explained. "I've been prepping for this for years, because I knew it would come. I knew one day the world was going to go to hell – and now it has. Now only the strong and the prepared will survive. Now the weak and infirm will be the first to die. I didn't cause the situation, but I ain't going to be a victim, so don't give me your bleeding heart shit. I ain't got time. None of us have."

Cutter said nothing for a long moment. He could hear women talking urgently on their phones, and the sound of running water coming from the lunch room. "You think you're prepared for this?"

"As well as can be," Hos said confidently. "I've got guns, ammunition and enough survival gear in my bug-out bag to make it out of the city and get clear to safety."

"Enough gear for you. Right?"

Hos nodded. "For me."

Cutter raised an eyebrow. "Then what happens to the rest of us?"

"I don't give a shit," Hos flared. "You should have thought of that before doomsday. Right now you're safe. But once we leave this place, you, and the rest of these people are on your own," he said bluntly.

"You're just going to leave us? Abandon everyone in this room?"

"Damned right I am," Hos said, and his voice became an angry growl. "I came into town to fetch my mother from the nursing home because I thought there was still time. But when I got there she was crawling across the floor, vomiting blood and moaning like a mad fuckin' dog," he snarled. "So I put a bullet in her head. Then I came in to work to get my bug out bag, and got caught here. I should have been away by now."

"Away? Away where?" Cutter was confused. "Where is there to go?"

"I've got a place. About forty miles out of town."

"A place?"

"A compound. On some land. That's where I'm going. That's where I'll wait this thing out," Hos explained.

Cutter frowned. "What makes your place any safer than any other?"

"Because I've prepared," Hos said. "I've got enough weapons and ammunition to last six months, a motorbike, and months of food and bottled water. And I've got a small generator. It's the kind of place that doesn't get noticed. And it's isolated from other properties."

"But there's no hope for the rest of these people?"

"Probably not."

"Then why did you save them?" Cutter was suddenly angry. He felt his resentment rise, and he clenched his fists. "Why did you save me? Why are you doing what you're doing right now?"

"Because it serves my interests," Hos snapped. "I'm trapped here. Until I make a break for it, there's safety and support in numbers. Simple. But once I'm on the move, every one of you becomes a liability. You're dead weight around my neck. Every one of you. It ain't gonna happen."

Cutter looked away for a moment, and when he turned back his eyes were dark and repulsed. "I called you a murderer," he said levelly. "And I meant it. This is just murder in another form. Either way, we're all dead."

"Not me."

Cutter glared. "Then at least tell these people right now what they're up against," he urged. "Tell them what their chances are and what you're planning. Tell them they're on their own when they leave this place because they think you're going to lead them! They're counting on you already. I've seen it in their faces. They think you're going to lead them to safety – not abandon them when they've ceased being any use to you. You owe them that. You owe them the chance to make their own decisions, and their own preparations, dammit."

"To hell with them," Hos snapped coldly. "I told you only the strong are going to survive. I've got my own agenda. I'm not planning on being slowed down by any passengers."

Cutter seized the man's shoulder. "They're women, for God's sake! They're your workmates and friends," he snapped. "They need your help."

"Fuck 'em," Hos said coldly. His eyes were flinty hard and merciless. He shook Cutter's hand from his shoulder. "I'm the dispatch guy. I work down here sending books round the country. That's all. I'm not anyone's friend."

"You're not a dispatch guy anymore. Not as far as these people are concerned. You're their only hope, man. You're their one chance at survival."

"That's not my choice. Not my decision."

"It is, dammit," Cutter's anger flared white-hot. "It became your decision when you said you were taking over. It became your decision when you told that poor woman none of them could leave to reach their families, and when you organized everyone into tasks."

The big man's face turned to stone. Cutter could sense his fury. Hos's lips became thin bloodless lines across his dark face, and his fists bunched into shapes like massive hammers.

"Fine," Hos snapped suddenly. "I'll fix that right now."

He stormed back into the kitchen area and dropped the semi-automatic rifle on the table with a clatter so loud that the women in the room jumped with fright and fell suddenly silent. Hos put his hands on his hips, looming over them like an avalanche of angry muscle, and when he spoke his voice was pitched low and rumbling.

"I'm not leading you out of here," he declared. "When we break out, I'm travelling on my own. I want you to know that right now. So if you're looking to me to save you, you are looking at the wrong man. You need to save yourselves. Make your own plans, make your own choices. Once we leave this bunker, you'll never see me again."

For long seconds the room was shocked and silent. "So if you're looking for a savior, I'm not it. Maybe Mr. Grainger will take you with him. Or

56

maybe this guy," Hos pointed at Cutter. "But I won't."

Cutter took a sudden step back as desperate eyes turned to him in hope and expectation. He shook his head. "I'm not fit to lead. And I don't want the responsibility," he said darkly. "I'm a commercial artist, not a survivalist. I've never fired a gun in my life."

Cutter glared at Hos. The big man glared back. The tension between them crackled in the air like electricity. Finally Hos snatched up the rifle from the table and stooped to pick up the nylon bag. He stormed back out into the gloomy warehouse. Cutter stood for a moment longer, seeing the sudden spark of hope in the eyes of the gathered women fade, then die completely, and the sickened despair in their expressions made him wonder whether he had been right to confront Hos at all.

Maybe it would have been better to let everyone cling to hope that Hos would save them – even if that hope was false. Maybe he should have kept his mouth shut until he knew more about what was happening in the streets overhead. He stared at the women silently for long seconds, then went after Hos, back out into the warehouse.

The big man was waiting for him, sitting hunched against a concrete wall. He had the nylon bag open between his feet, and the rifle propped against the wall beside him. Cutter stood, watching until Hos looked up and met his gaze. There was a black pistol in one of the big man's hands.

"This is a Glock 19," Hos said. It was a compact, sleek looking weapon. "It's loaded with a full magazine. That's fifteen rounds." He held the weapon out. Cutter took the handgun reluctantly.

"All you've got to do is pull the slide back and let it slam forward. Then point it at one of the undead fucker's heads, and pull the trigger."

Cutter felt the weight of the weapon and was surprised at how comfortably and balanced it sat in his hand. He turned it over. "Isn't there supposed to be some kind of a safety switch on guns?"

Hos shook his head. "Not on the Glock," he said. "Just pull the trigger. The safety on these things is in the take-up."

Cutter shook his head. "What are you giving it to me for?" he asked. "I told you I've never fired a gun in my life."

"You'll need it."

Cutter's tone was icy. "Don't do me any favors."

Hos grunted. "I'm not," he said bluntly. "I'm making you useful – because right now you're not. You're nothing but a useless drain on supplies and resources. That's the only reason you get the gun," he said. "You're pulling sentry duty. Grainer and the kid too. The three of you will alternate between guarding the steel door and the shipping door tonight, so you'll need a gun – just in case."

Cutter nodded. Said nothing.

Hos zipped the nylon bag closed and got to his feet. "Don't point that thing at anything you don't intend to kill, and keep your fucking finger off the trigger till you're ready to fire," he warned Cutter. "And don't try to shoot any of those undead fuckers unless you're less than six feet away. You've never fired a gun before, so you're going to miss with a head shot unless they're breathing down your neck."

Cutter nodded. He tucked the weapon inside the waistband of his jeans.

And then both men heard a sudden shout, coming from the lunchroom. One of the women was screaming, her voice rising hysterical and panic-stricken.

Cutter and Hos started running.

* * *

The women still in the lunchroom were gathered around the television. Hos and Cutter shouldered their way through the group. A lady was laying on her back on the cement floor, legs outstretched, her breathing shallow but regular. One of the other women was kneeling over her with the unconscious woman's head in her lap.

"She collapsed," the woman looked up at Cutter and Hos, then pointed at the television, as though it was the cause of the turmoil. "I think she's fainted."

The two men's eyes snapped to the screen.

A station logo was dissolving, replaced by a wide-angled view of a street. The camera had been positioned somewhere overhead – maybe on top of a deserted nearby building. The elevated angle showed a group of about a hundred heavily armed riot police, standing in two thin lines. The men were wearing bulky black uniforms, helmets and full-face gas masks, braced in a human wall behind bullet-proof shields. Behind the ranks of police were several heavy vans, like armored cars, and a couple of parked up buses, their windows barred and blacked out.

Stretched out before the intimidating show of police resistance was a length of road, littered with burning vehicles and debris. Cutter saw the grainy image of a police car that had been overturned. The windows were shattered and blood-spattered. Nearby was a small compact sedan, standing in the middle of the blacktop as a charred burned out shell. Smoke and billowing clouds of white gas turned the air into a haze.

Then the camera moved, panning urgently towards an intersection where a horde of crazed, blood-drenched undead were shambling in a solid wave towards where the police line waited. The camera swept across the grotesque faces and their horrible disfigurements, and then went back to a wide shot.

Cutter sensed the anxiety of the women around him. It seemed as though everyone in the room was holding their breath.

A man's voice, shaky and uncertain, cut in over the sounds of the moaning wave of terror.

"These shots are live from the outskirts of Baltimore," the announcer explained. *"Where police and the army have drawn up a last-ditch defensive line against the plague of infected..."*

The voice-over cut off abruptly, and the announcer's image appeared in a corner of the screen. Cutter drew his eyes back to the main picture and saw the crowd swelling as it drew closer to the line of police. Then, as if let off some unholy leash, the front rank of the marauding undead suddenly broke from a shamble and began swarming towards the blockade.

"Sweet Jesus," Hos breathed, and despite the drama being played out live before their terrified eyes, every face in the room turned to look at the big survivalist. "They're running," he said, and there was a dark, appalled sense of awe in his tone. "They're not staggering. They're not lurching. Some of those fuckers are running!"

Cutter looked back to the television urgently. About fifty of the undead were sprinting towards the police line. They were snarling: possessed by some mindless maddening rage that hurled them at the wall of riot shields in a frenzy. Behind them, the rest of the undead mass was splintering into fragments as those who could move faster began to break from the seething undulating body of the horde.

The sound rose to a wail, reaching a crescendo at the instant before the first undead slammed into the blockade.

The police braced themselves – set their legs and their balance to absorb the impact – but the collision was so violent the wall instantly began to buckle inwards. Cutter watched in horror. The police were hammering at bloody, snarling faces with their batons, and for one brief moment it seemed as though the blockade would hold, as the surging tide of ghouls crashed against the shields and was repulsed.

The zombies drew back like a tide, and then hurled themselves forward again, this time their savage madness reinforced by the weight of those heaving from behind. They fell against the wall of riot police, demented and relentless.

Then one of the undead broke through the interlocking shields, flailing its arms and snapping its infected jaws like a rabid dog into the uniformed bodies. A whistle sounded, and there was the dull percussive sound of tear gas being fired into the swarm. But it was no use. The crack became a breach, and the wall lost its integrity – and with it all chance of survival. One of the cops reeled away, flinging down his riot shield and clutching at his neck. He wrenched off his gas mask and helmet, and his face was a rictus of agonized pain, as he sagged to his knees. That was all it took. Zombies stormed through the narrow fissure, gnashing and tearing at the riot police. The line fractured. From off camera a dozen more black-uniformed troopers raced frantically to fill the gap, but it was too late. The defensive wall of police protection dissolved in a seething maelstrom of blood and horror.

Most of the police died where they stood. Others tried to flee and were hunted down and savaged. Then a storm of automatic gunfire erupted. The camera jerked out of focus, then centered on an army vehicle. It was a troop carrier with slab-sides, and rolling steel tracks like a tank. It was painted in a drab camouflage of greens and browns, and there was a heavy machine gun mounted on top of the vehicle. A goggled, helmeted soldier was swinging the weapon in a sweeping arc across the street, ripping a hail of murderous gunfire into the zombies.

The vehicle lurched, then surged forward on its tracks, bulldozing into the horde with a sound like rolling thunder. Machine gun fire ripped a swathe through the mass of wailing ghouls. Cutter saw bodies ripped apart and flung aside like debris. The undead caught in the murderous fire seemed to fold backwards as though cut down by a scythe.

The vehicle churned up the road, it's heavy tracks gouging into the asphalt as it shouldered ruined cars aside. The swarm parted and swirled around it like a storm surge dashing against rocks.

Then the machine gun fire stopped suddenly, and Cutter saw the sudden panic of the man behind the weapon.

Those undead who had been left destroyed under the tracks of the vehicle and maimed by the savage burst of gunfire began to rise slowly up from the road, their movements slowed, but still driven with the same blind rage.

Behind him, Cutter heard one of the women gasp.

In another instant it was all over. The undead rushed up and over the sides of the vehicle and clawed at the soldier behind the machine gun. He flailed out with his fists, and then fell into the surging crowd, screaming in terror. The camera jerked again, and then zoomed close. The image became grainy, but not so obscured that Cutter couldn't see three of the undead hurl themselves down through the open hatch of the armored vehicle.

The camera cut away suddenly, and the image returned to the announcer in the studio. The man's face was ashen. He stared at the screen for long seconds of shocked, grieving silence, and when he finally spoke his voice was heavy. He looked down at a sheath of typed notes clutched in his hands.

"Repeating the news from earlier..." he said slowly. *"A state of Martial Law has been declared across the eastern seaboard of the United States. Speaking from a secured bunker earlier today, the President confirmed that the military has been issued executive orders to shoot to kill anyone on the streets. Citizens are advised to remain in doors and all air traffic across the country has been grounded indefinitely by the FAA."* The man paused, then looked back to the screen. *"There is a total blockade*

on all civilian vehicular movement, and the military is drawing a defensive line from Chicago in the north through St Louis, to Memphis, to New Orleans in the south, called Line 55. Those west of the I-55 Interstate are urged to avoid all contact with anyone wounded or presenting symptoms of abnormal behavior, and to report any suspicious activity immediately to authorities. Those people still alive east of the Chicago-New Orleans infection line are urged to seek the safety of any nearby military installations that may be operational. You are warned not to attempt to reach the defensive line being set up by the military. Repeat: do not attempt to approach the defensive containment barrier. Anyone approaching the I-55 Containment line from the east will be shot and killed."

Cutter turned slowly away from the television, while behind him, the screen filled with fresh images showing army helicopters airlifting huge iron pylons and concrete slabs.

"It's the Berlin Wall all over again," one of the older women in the group said softly. "They're building a wall and abandoning us."

Below the transport helicopters, long snaking lines of army trucks were winding their way across deserted roads, kicking up clouds of dust across the horizon, while sleek helicopter gunships swarmed through the sky. Tanks took up positions blocking arterial freeways, hull-down behind concrete barriers.

Cutter went to the tiny sink and drank a glass of water. All the coffee was gone. When he turned back, Hos was changing channels on the television, scrolling through hissing static until he found another station that was still broadcasting. Two women reporters were sitting stiffly at a news presenter's desk and behind them was a graphic showing three army tanks and the legend 'Line 55' in large red lettering.

One of the women was reading from a teleprompter, while the other stared numbly at the camera.

The graphic behind the presenters changed suddenly to an all-yellow screen with several lines of bold black type.

"Here's what we now know," the announcer began expanding on each of the points that were showing on the screen. *"The infection is a virus, and at this stage there is no known antidote. The virus is one hundred percent fatal. The virus is spread through bites and exposure to infected saliva or blood. Once infected, the dead re-animate – yes reanimate – within three to eight minutes."* There was a long pause, before the woman continued to the second point. *"It has been confirmed that the infected become faster once the virus has fully taken over their body. Initial reports of the undead moving slowly have now been refuted by several incidents in Virginia, Pennsylvania and New York over the past few hours. Those still living east of Line 55 are urged to take extreme caution and should avoid areas of dense population wherever possible."*

The woman went through the rest of the list but Cutter was barely listening. He heard the woman mention that the undead seemed to be aroused and enraged by noise, but little else until she came to the final point.

"President Sharpe has promised full and violent retribution should the spread of the virus be proven to be a terrorist attack on America," she said. *"At*

this stage the government has not ruled out the possibility but remains guarded and cautious. So far eighteen terrorist organizations have claimed responsibility for the plague. Government investigations are said to be continuing, alongside the largest peace-time mobilization of military and civilian forces in the nation's history."

The screen cut to a grab of the President, standing at a lectern. There was a blue curtain behind him. At the President's shoulder stood several grim-faced men in uniforms. Cutter stopped listening. Presidential messages of hope and promise weren't going to change the situation or alter the reality.

They had been left to die.

* * *

Cutter lost all sense of time. Under the artificial light, every moment was the same, so he was surprised when the blonde woman he had first seen behind the steel door drifted out from the kitchen area carrying two glasses of water.

"It's eight o'clock," she said. "I thought you might like a drink."

Cutter nodded. The woman sat down on the hard concrete floor beside him and leaned her back against the brick wall. She watched Cutter sip at the water and smiled wanly.

Cutter studied the woman over the rim of his glass as he drank. She had fixed her hair, and washed her face. Her eyes were still red and puffy, but she had touched at her features with makeup in some small gesture of vanity.

She was pretty, Cutter realized. He guessed that she was in her late twenties. She had long blonde hair that spilled over her shoulders in a cascade of curls, and enormous green eyes. Her features were petite, her mouth wide, her body slim and with a lithe athleticism that suggested long hours in a gym.

Cutter smiled back at the woman, and set the glass down.

He was hunched against the wall, using his pocket-knife to whittle the length of a broom handle down to a point. He had two other makeshift spears already completed. He stretched the cramped muscles across his back and shoulders.

The woman held out her hand. "Glenda," she said softly.

"Cutter. Jack Cutter."

The woman's hand was small and delicate. She had long sculptured fingers and nails that were painted pink. Her skin was smooth and soft, but her grip was surprisingly firm.

The others in the group had drifted to all parts of the warehouse. Several women remained in the lunchroom, seated around the table. The television had been turned off, but the women sat chatting in a desultory hush, perhaps drawn by the comfort of the bright overhead lights. Others had taken books from the shelves and sat in quiet corners reading. John Grainger was pacing the room, walking between the rows of high dusty bookcases, measuring each step as though the monotony of walking was a hedge against his panic, while by the boarded-up shipping door at the rear of the building, Jimmy was preparing more weapons. Apart from the hammers, he had found a fire-axe and a short lump of lead pipe that he hefted like a club.

Cutter watched them with a kind of detached fascination. Every person was handling the crisis in their own way, internalizing their fears and panic – blocking out the nightmare images – and trying to ward off the crushing despair of hopelessness that seemed to fill the very air.

Only Hos seemed to be driven by a purpose.

The big man was sitting at the foot of the stairs that led up to the steel door. He had the black bag at his feet, quietly going through the contents, checking and re-checking equipment. In the gloomy lighting he was just a vague shape, but every once in a while Cutter sensed the survivalist's eyes upon him – watching him in stealthy, brooding silence from the darkness.

Cutter turned back to the woman. She was sitting close beside him – so close that he could sense the warmth of her body and smell the faint lingering muskiness of her perfume. She had her head tilted back against the wall, her eyes closed in an attitude of weary fatigue, exposing the long soft lines of her throat. She had unfastened the top button of her blouse, and as Cutter followed the line of her neck, he could see a glimpse of pale cleavage. He looked away and stared fixedly off into space, then sighed.

"I never dreamed this day would come," he said softly. "I just never thought it could ever happen."

He sensed the woman's eyes opening and her face turning to him. "None of us did," she said softly. "There have been so many predictions about the end of the world. Who would ever have thought it would come unannounced, and without any time to prepare?"

Cutter grinned wryly. "Hos," he said. "He's a survivalist. The bastard has been waiting for this day to come. It's the moment he has spent his life preparing for."

Glenda nodded slowly. "When he first started work here at the bookstore, he used to creep me out," she confessed in a whisper. "Just the way he acted and the things he said. All he ever talked about was guns, you know," she shrugged. "I thought he was going to end up on the news – one of those crazy guys holed up in a house somewhere surrounded by police cars." The thought made her giggle, and the sound was such a shock that Cutter turned to her so their faces were just inches apart.

"Well he's the one who is laughing now," Cutter whispered. "He's the one guy we need to have any chance of surviving Armageddon – and he's the only one who doesn't need any of us to help him."

Cutter's thoughts drifted back to the horror of the day and he felt a cold sense of clammy despair clutch at his heart. Was their really any point in trying to survive? Why couldn't he just lie down and die – maybe end it all right now by chewing on a bullet?

He closed his eyes and asked softly, "Did you have family?"

"No," Glenda said sadly. "Not really. I was an orphan. I lived with a foster family in Omaha until I was seventeen. Then I moved here to find work..." her voice drifted to silence for a wistful moment. "There were a couple of guys... but nothing serious." She shifted her weight subtly, until her shoulder was brushing against his. Cutter didn't move, but he felt a sudden sense of intimacy.

"How about you? Did you lose anyone?" Glenda asked him softly. "Do you have family nearby?"

Cutter thought about how to answer. It was a simple question, but for Jack Cutter, the answer was darkly complicated. He nodded slowly. "I lost my wife and my son," he said. "But not to the virus. They were killed in a car crash last week."

He heard Glenda gasp softly. "Oh, God. I'm so sorry," she said, and Cutter believed her. "Was... was it an accident?"

Cutter nodded, and felt the crushing despair and misery of his loss well up until it was like a knot in his chest. "Yes," he said. "I was driving. It was late at night. A dog ran out on the road. I swerved..."

"But you survived."

"Yes. Not a scratch on me, but my wife and son were so horribly crushed and disfigured I could barely recognize the bodies."

They stared at each other in the gloom for long uncertain seconds of silence and anguish, and then a sudden movement caught in the corner of Cutter's eye made him turn away. One of the other women who worked in the bookstore was walking past them, her heels loud and echoing in the sullen silence. She was a tall woman, very young. She walked with her back straight, thrusting her breasts out firm against the fabric of her blouse. She had long red hair. She sensed Cutter watching her and she gave him a lingering glance as she passed. Cutter felt Glenda's hand on his forearm.

"I'm not surprised," Glenda whispered, and there was a harsh sound of distain in her voice. "If anyone was going to try it, I knew it would be that little slut."

Cutter frowned. "Try it?"

Glenda followed the younger woman with her eyes, tracking her as she sauntered towards where Hos sat on the steps. "She's going to make a play for Hos in the hope he will take her with him when we break out of here."

Cutter shook his head. "You're fucking joking!"

Glenda sniffed. "It takes a woman to know a woman," she said with a kind of abstractness that Cutter didn't follow. "Jillian is just doing what a lot of the others have already considered."

Glenda's words hung in the air for a long moment. Cutter turned back to her slowly. "Including you...?"

Glenda didn't answer. She glanced towards the stairs. Jillian was standing in front of Hos, leaning against the railing with her other hand resting on her narrow waist. Her hips were tilted at a sensual angle so that her skirt pulled tight across the shape of her thighs and bottom. As Glenda and Cutter watched, Hos muttered something and Jillian leaned closer to the man and then nodded her head willingly.

Glenda turned back to Cutter. She sighed. "I don't blame her..." she began, and then shook her head and started again. "You know, we think we're civilized. We think we've evolved in the thousands of years man has walked the earth. Women have more independence and have been completely empowered – and yet – within twenty four hours of the world going to hell, we revert back to those base animal instincts that we've always inherited but learned to suppress," she said. "Like the instinctive need to find a mate, and to reproduce, the instinct to survive is the strongest one mankind has, and Jillian is just doing what women have done for thousands of years. She's drawn to the strongest male because it's her best chance of protection and survival – and she's appealing to him in the one way men are instinctively created to respond. She's offering him her body, in the hope he will want her and will protect her. It's what every woman instinctively craves," Glenda confessed.

"Including you..." Cutter said again, this time not asking the question. Just stating the fact.

Glenda sighed. "I'd be lying if I told you I wasn't jealous," she admitted. "Like you said, Hos is the one person in this room who is prepared for what is happening. It makes him the dominant male. Instinctively, he's drawing every woman in here towards him."

"And so why are you talking to me?" Cutter asked. His tone had suddenly become harsh. "Why aren't you lifting your skirt to Hos and throwing yourself at him? Or did you realize Hos would choose one of the younger girls, and so you thought maybe I would be your second choice?"

Glenda turned away for a moment, and when she looked back there was a flicker of venomous anger in her eyes. Cutter saw the conflict in her expression flare brightly and then turn cold.

"Would it make any difference?" she said flatly, grinding down on her urge to stalk angrily away. "You decide. If you want me, you can have me. You can take me right here, right now. You can take me up against the wall and I don't care if everyone else in the room sees." She snatched at his hand and the look in her eyes was urgent and primitive. "I want to survive this," she said. "I'm too young to die. I've got my whole life ahead of me and I want to live it, no matter how horrible the world becomes." Her legs fell apart, and she slid Cutter's hand up under her skirt and held it pressed against the soft damp silk of her panties. "Take me with you, Jack. Promise you'll protect me, and I'll be yours any time you want. Every time you want. That's what I'm prepared to pay for you to get me out of here and keep me alive."

Cutter recoiled. He dragged his hand free and glared, his expression appalled. Glenda started crying soft tears of despair and humiliation. She jerked away from him. "I'm sorry," she said in a tiny choking sound. "I... I've done this all wrong..." She covered her mouth and began to sob. Cutter sat frozen, watching the woman's pain. Over her shoulder, in the gloomy distance, he saw Hos take the young redhead by the hand and lead her away towards one of the small storage spaces. He hunted the darkness with his eyes until the couple disappeared.

When his eyes flicked back to Glenda, she was hunched against the wall, her body shaking and heaving with the depth of her desolation. Finally he reached for her. Drew her close to him and she looked up into his face with meek, fragile hope.

"Thank you, Jack," she whispered urgently. Her hand went to the front of his jeans in a desperate flurry to please him. "I promise I'll be everything you want," she said. "I promise you can have me whenever you say." Her fingers were practiced, and with quick movements she unbuttoned the denim and began drawing down the zipper. She felt the hardness of him.

Cutter grabbed her wrist. "Not that," he said, and shook his head firmly. "Not anything." Glenda's head was nestled against his chest. She looked up at him, her eyes wide in alarm and renewed fear. "But —"

Cutter shook his head again. "Just lay still, and get some rest," he said. "I'm sorry. But for now, comfort is all I can offer you."

* * *

Rough hands shook him awake and Cutter sat up with a start. Hos was standing over him, leaning close so that his voice was just a whisper.

"It's midnight," the big man said. His eyes drifted down to where Glenda was laying with her head resting in Cutter's lap. The woman was breathing steadily, but shallowly, her brow creased into a furrow as she slept. Hos said nothing, but there was a knowing look in his eyes. He grunted. "You've got sentry duty at the steel door. I'll relieve you at 4am."

Cutter nodded. His hand went to the bulky shape of the pistol that had jammed itself against his hip as he had slept. "Okay," he said.

Hos leaned an inch closer. "Stay the fuck awake," he warned, his voice pitched low, but full of menace.

* * *

Cutter climbed the stairs and sat on the cold concrete of the landing with his back against the locked steel door. He felt numb with the weary fatigue of exhaustion, and his thoughts were chittering and inconsequential.

It was as though his mind had finally shut down, denying him the ability to think clearly. The enormity of the peril – America on the brink of Armageddon – had forced his conscious mind into denial.

Or maybe it was simply that there was no point in thinking, or planning for anything beyond the first few moments after they pulled open the steel door...

But Cutter was used to that. He was used to living one moment at a time, and staring into an uncertain future that seemed to have no consequence and no reason.

Ever since his wife and son had died...

* * *

He heard the soft shuffle of cautious steps, and for a split second he wondered whether the sound was vibrating through the thick steel door. Then he saw Hos at the bottom of the stairs. The big man had the semi-automatic cradled in his arms, and the black nylon bag strapped to his back. His eyes were bright and alert.

He looked up at Cutter and touched at his wrist; signaling that it was time. Cutter came down the steps. Hos put his hand out for the Glock.

Cutter felt strangely disquieted relinquishing the gun. There was some tangible sense of safety in its weight and when he gave the weapon back to Hos it was with a pang of reluctance.

"It's 4am," Hos said. "Go and get some sleep. You'll need it in the morning."

Cutter nodded. He stood at the bottom of the steps for another moment, watching the big survivalist take the stairs up to the narrow landing, and then finally trudged back into the gloom of the warehouse where the rest of the group slept fitfully on the edge of nightmare.

* * *

"Jack! Jesus, Jack! Get up. Please get up!"

Cutter came awake resentfully, aware of someone tugging and shaking him – aware also of some dull sense of brooding remorse. He felt agitated hands plucking at his arm until he came alert blinking and ill-tempered.

He dragged his hand across the unshaven stubble of his jaw. "What time is it?"

"Almost seven am," Glenda's face hovered above him. Her eyes were huge and haunted.

Cutter blinked again. Other women were crowded around where he lay, peering over Glenda's shoulder. Cutter sat up.

"It's Hos," Glenda said, her voice trembling with outrage. "He's gone. He must have left in the night," she said in a rush of words. "The bastard has abandoned us."

* * *

They were assembled in the lunchroom. No one sat. They were too fraught and too distressed by Hos's betrayal. Instead, they lined the wall like timid victims awaiting the blade of the executioner.

Cutter strode into the room. He had left Jimmy on sentry duty at the top of the landing, armed with the fire axe.

John Grainger was slumped nearest the door. His features seemed to have sagged with the strain, so that the flesh around his beefy cheeks and eyes hung in soft grey pouches. He glanced up as Cutter entered, and the two men exchanged brief glances.

"We have no food left," Cutter said simply. "What little there was is now gone. We have fresh water, a few wooden spears and an axe. That's it – and it's not going to get any better," he said. He glanced at John Grainger again and it seemed clear to the women in the room that the two men had talked before this meeting, and that they were of differing opinions.

"I think we should leave now," Cutter said. "Mr. Grainger thinks we should wait another day or two." He shrugged. "The choice is your own to make."

Cutter went to the small refrigerator and snatched up a plastic bottle of water. "I'm taking this," he said. "I suggest anyone else who decides to leave takes all the water they can carry. You'll need it."

Around him the women erupted into sudden heated panic. "Grainger is right!" he heard someone cry out, loud and plaintive. He recognized the voice. It was the woman who had fainted yesterday. She was one of the older women in the group, a small, frail shape with lank grey hair. "We should wait it out. We've contacted the police. They'll come for us! I know they will."

Other voices joined the call, but Glenda shouted them down. She stood defiant, her hands on her hips, turning on them, her eyes cold as ice. "No one is coming for us, Jennifer. No one. You know it. I know it. We all know it. We can't wait here and pray for rescue. If we do, we're as good as dead already."

John Grainger shook his head. "We're safe while we stay here," he challenged Glenda, his voice wilting a little under the force of her defiant glare. He plowed on, like a train running out of steam. "They... the infected can't... and in a few days, who knows what might happen..."

Glenda's lips drew back into a thin, pale sneer. "We can't wait," she said again. "There's no food, and there's something else you've forgotten," she said archly. Before anyone could take up her challenge, she strode to the wall and flicked off the lights. The entire basement was plunged into heavy, terrifying darkness. One of the women cried out, and after a few seconds Glenda turned the lights back on. She glared at them all. "Any moment, the power is going to fail," she said. "Think about that, and decide whether you can spend two or three days hiding down here in the pitch black. Because I can't. I'm going – not because I want to – because there is no other choice. And if we wait another minute, it won't get any better. But it might get worse..."

The uncertain amongst the group turned towards Grainger, looking for guidance and reassurance, but the store manager had been shaken by the few seconds of total darkness. He buried his hands in his face and sagged forward, and when he finally drew himself upright again, his eyes were red and watery. He nodded. "Okay," he said and took a deep breath. "Okay. It's time to make a break for safety."

Cutter nodded. He set the bottle of water down on the table and cast his eyes around the room once more. "When we get out onto the street, you should look for a way to reach the outer suburbs," he said. "You've all heard the broadcast warnings. The infected will be worse in the city, so get away as far as you can. There will be hundreds of abandoned cars. That might be your best chance..." but then his voice faltered. He shook his head in bleak despair. "I honestly don't know what's best," he admitted. "I just know what I'm going to try to do."

"You're abandoning us too? Just like Hos?" one of the women accused, her voice made small by her fear.

Cutter shook his head. "I said yesterday that I wasn't the man to lead," he replied. "I've never fired a gun, and I've never been in the military. I'm not the person you should put your faith in. I'm sorry," he said.

Glenda grabbed his arm. "You're our best chance!"

There was a long tense silence. Cutter frowned, feeling the crushing weight of people's expectations that he knew were impossible to live up to. His eyes searched the faces of those around him and he could see their desperate need for hope. "I'll take four of you," he said at last. "As far as I can. If Mr. Grainger and Jimmy agree, they will each take four women in their group as well. That makes three teams – three chances of surviving."

All eyes turned to John Grainger, desperate hopes pinned on his answer. He nodded reluctantly.

"But I'm going first," Cutter said, "and I'm going now. At least in small groups we have a chance of finding a vehicle and getting away," he was talking aloud, making desperate plans based on nothing more than instinct. "And I want the fastest runners – the fittest women," he said. "With any luck, if there are zombies still out there, we can lead them away." He turned to John Grainger again. "Give me thirty minutes, then take your group out," he said. "Tell Jimmy to do the same. Tell him to wait thirty minutes after you leave here before he takes the last group out."

Cutter pulled Glenda aside, and thrust a small water bottle into her hand. Then he nodded at Jillian and two of the other younger bookstore employees. "You're coming with me," he said grimly. "Now."

Waiting even another minute would give him time to think, and time to re-consider. Cutter knew he couldn't afford the luxury. He simply wasn't brave enough. Now his mind was made up, he needed to move quickly, before second thoughts and fear debilitated them. He snatched up one of the broom-handle spears, and the four women followed him from the lunchroom in single file.

Three.
Ground Zero.

Cutter pushed at the big steel door with his foot and it swung back silently on massive steel hinges.

He stood in the breech, every muscle in his body tensed, every nerve strained to breaking point. He had the spear held at waist height, clutched in both hands, and his knuckles were white.

He blinked, eyes adjusting to the dull natural light, and all his senses were enhanced. He could smell a sweet putrid odor, and he could smell smoke, lingering in the air. He felt a breath of breeze on his face, and then a trickle of nervous sweat ran down his back. He forced himself to take a step into the bookstore, his stomach tripping with an instinctive animal sense of danger that warned him something lurked nearby.

He took another step, and then another. Then he paused, frozen, as his eyes swept past the gloomy bookshelves around him.

He turned back to the open door. Nodded. Glenda and the other women came from the landing, huddled in a tight knot. One of the women was sobbing softly. She had her hand to her mouth to stifle the sound. Behind the group, John Grainger stood at the steel door. Cutter made eye contact with the man over the shoulders of the women. Cutter nodded. Grainger nodded back, and then without another word, he pulled the steel door slowly closed and locked it from the inside.

The sound of the door shutting was nothing more than a faint 'snick', yet to Cutter it sounded like the tolling bell of doom. The finality of it shocked him as he realized that now there was no turning back – no possible means of escape. The only way left was forward into a world he was unprepared for.

The bookstore was eerily quiet. Cutter led the women down the long passage towards the front door, his eyes never resting, never focusing on one point. His head swept across every shelf and every display stand, and the tension rose with each step that drew them closer to the street until he could smell their rising fear.

They crept past the cashier's counter, and paused. Ahead of them, Cutter could see piled tangles of furniture and overturned bookshelves that had formed part of the barricade the day earlier. The store's display window had been shattered, and jagged shards of glass and crumpled paperbacks lay like litter on the floor. He stepped carefully, his eyes sweeping the street beyond.

It was a clear sunny day. He could see burned and crumpled cars choking all three lanes of the road. Further away – on the opposite side of the street – he saw a tall black pyre of smoke billowing from the smashed windows of a women's dress store. And dead on the ground were dozens of broken, lifeless bodies, and grotesque streaks of blood that were spattered across the pavement like outraged graffiti.

Cutter turned back to the women and pointed to a breach in the barricade where a desk had been overturned and one of the destroyed bookcases had fallen across the walkway. "Through there," he whispered. When the women nodded, he went forward slowly, measuring each and every step, his body crouched and alert.

He reached the broken furniture and paused, his sense of alarm suddenly heightened. From somewhere close by he heard soft scrabbling sounds. He froze for long seconds. The sound stopped, and then came again. Cutter held his breath. The stench of death was stronger now that they were approaching the doors of the store, carried in the smoky haze that drifted across the street. But with it was another smell – an odor that was somehow familiar. Cutter stepped cautiously into the narrow gap and stared towards the entrance of the bookstore.

And froze in cold stomach-churning shock.

Hos was lying dead on the floor, his arms flung wide, his upper body twisted at an angle by the bug-out bag that was still strapped to his back.

Crouched on the dead man's chest were two large rats.

Cutter felt an icy pall of dread wash over him as the blood drained away from his face. His head filled with a roar of noise, and for just a moment his vision blurred and he felt himself swaying. Behind him he heard Glenda gasp and whisper, "Oh, God!"

Cutter went forward. The rats were huge black beasts, their fur stiff dark bristles. They were feasting on Hos's guts, tearing and gnawing at the wet flesh of his entrails with razor sharp teeth as Cutter watched on in horror. One of the rats sensed Cutter and stared with evil yellow eyes. Its mouth was sticky with fresh blood, it's body hunched as though it might leap at him.

Cutter lunged forward with the spear and the rat snarled at him, baring wicked incisors. Cutter changed his grip on the spear and hefted it over his head, swinging down hard and smashing the huge growling rodent's spine. The rat squealed, and the sound was a high-pitched piercing wail. Cutter swung the spear again, this time side-armed, but missed. He raised the spear over his head once more and lunged down. The point drove through the rat's back and killed it in a gout of spraying warm blood as the rodent twisted and writhed like a fish on the end of a line.

Cutter swung the spear and flung the rat's body across the bookstore. The second rat defiantly burrowed it's snout deep into Hos's stomach cavity and ripped a long shred of flesh from the body's intestines. Its head came up covered in thick slimy gore. Then it scampered away into the shadows.

Cutter went down on one knee beside Hos's body. He was trembling. He felt a surge of nausea scald the back of his throat and had to bite down on the urge to gag. He covered his mouth with one hand to mask the overpowering stench.

Hos's features had been eaten away. Both of his eyes were gone. So were his lips and nose, leaving his face a bloody ruin. Cutter could see deep claw and bite marks, still welling and oozing blood.

"Why hasn't he turned into one of them?" one of the women asked. She was a plain-looking girl in her early twenties. She had big dark eyes and stringy brown hair.

Cutter looked up at her. "Because he wasn't bitten," he said heavily. "He was shot."

There was a single bullet hole in Hos's forehead; a seeping hideous wound surrounded by tiny fragments of bone and grey ooze.

The semi-automatic rifle was lying close beside the body. Hos's fingers had been gnawed down to ragged stumps of flesh. Cutter picked up the weapon and handed it to Glenda. Then he felt for the nylon straps of the bug-out bag. He turned his head away. He could feel his fingers touch the wet oozing mush of the ravaged body, making his grip slick and slippery, but he persisted until the buckles were unfastened. He rolled the body onto its side and dragged the bag free. He handed the bag to Jillian, and then dug into the dead man's jeans and found his wallet. There were some bank notes, a credit card and a driver's license. Cutter stuffed the wallet into his pocket and then let the body roll onto its back again. He wiped his hands on the carpet, but the abattoir stench clung to him like a repulsive odor that seemed to permeate his clothes and the pores of his skin.

He stood slowly. "Can you use that thing?" Cutter asked Glenda. She was holding the rifle comfortably on her hip. She nodded. "It's an AR-15," she said. "And I can use it."

As if to demonstrate the point, she checked to see if the gun was on safe then turned the weapon and glanced into the chamber. Cutter watched, fascinated. "What are you doing?"

"I'm unlocking the bolt and pulling it out of battery so I can check the chamber for a round," Glenda said, her hand working with small deft movements. She released the magazine to check it was full before seating it back into place. "Do I have time for a function check?"

Cutter frowned. "I don't know what that is – but you don't have time. We don't have time for anything.

Cutter unzipped the nylon bag and rummaged through the contents. He saw a flashlight, matches, two bottles of water a knife and more. Then his fingers found the Glock that Hos had given him for sentry duty the evening before. He pulled back on the slide to chamber a round and then handed the bag back to Jillian. "The bag is your responsibility," Cutter said. "Guard it with your life."

Cutter went forward to the entrance of the bookstore at a low crouch and knelt behind the cover of a steel trolley that had been upended. The women filed forward and dropped to the ground behind him. Cutter scanned the sidewalk and the street carefully. He felt Glenda's shoulder press hard against his. She was on one knee close beside him, with the barrel of the AR-15 propped on the trolley's thick steel frame. Cutter glanced down and saw the long length of her thigh where the skirt had rucked up high around her waist.

She saw the fleeting direction of his eyes and she stared at him for a second in open invitation. "The offer still stands," she said softly. "Just take me with you, Jack."

Cutter said nothing. He tore his eyes from Glenda's and looked at the horror spread before him.

It was like a nightmare made real: a terrible, terrifying illusion turned into grotesque reality.

On the sidewalk, just beyond the shade of the bookstore's doorway, was the body of a woman. She was lying on her back, her body bloated and swollen. Her legs were askew, her arms out flung, and her head turned to the side so that she stared at Cutter with open, vacant eyes. Flies buzzed around the body in a thick angry swarm, laying eggs in the open wounds and crawling across her stricken face before disappeared inside the cavity of her mouth.

The woman's chest had been ripped open, and the soft flesh of her breasts ravaged and ripped from the corpse.

Beyond the woman's body was another, and another, appearing ghost-like and ethereal in the drifting haze of thick smoke that swirled on the gentle morning breeze.

Cutter tore his eyes away. The street appeared deserted. He searched the area again carefully, his eyes hunting through the scattered abandoned cars, looking for danger. But all he could see were more bodies. Some of them were slumped dead over the steering wheels of their vehicles. One man lay hanging out through the driver-side door of a grey hatchback, as though killed as he tried to flee the vehicle and make it to safety. The man's skull has been ripped away so that his face and the grey oozing contents of his head lay spattered on the tarmac.

And through the gore and smoke moved the scavenging dark shapes of rats and hulking awkward birds, picking at the pieces with macabre ravenous delight.

The bookstore was hemmed in on either side by other buildings. Cutter turned his head and looked towards either end of the street. Cars were crumpled ruined shapes across all three lanes of the blacktop. He saw sedans and SUV's flipped onto their sides. He saw other vehicles burned out. He saw cars with their doors open and others with their windows shattered, left skewed across the road during the last frantic moments before the world had been plunged into chaos.

He followed the road with his eyes towards the intersection – maybe sixty yards away – and through the smoke he saw the dark shadowed shapes of a couple of SUV's. The vehicles had been stopped at the traffic lights when the helicopters had appeared overhead, and the teeming mass of undead had stormed along the street.

He turned to the women and pointed. "We're going to head towards the traffic lights," he explained in a hush. "There's no way we'll get one of these closer cars through the wreckage. But if we can find a car close to the lights, we'll have a good chance of being able to shoulder our way through to open road. Then we'll head east and get as far out of the city as possible."

Cutter knew it wouldn't be as easy as he said. Between them and the safety of the city's outlying suburbs was a dozen arterial roads, and each of them would be jammed with the same choking chaos. But he plowed on, forcing the faintest hint of hope into his voice and noticing how the women responded, as though optimism was infectious. "Once we're out on the street, we go hard," he said. "Don't stop for anything. Just get to one of the cars and get the engine running."

He grabbed Glenda's shoulder. "You're in the lead," he said. "I'll be right behind you. If you see anything or anyone, shoot to kill. Don't think. Don't hesitate. Aim for the head and put them down. Understand?"

Glenda nodded. She swallowed hard – a convulsive nervous reaction – and then clenched her jaw grimly.

The clock in Cutter's head was ticking. He figured they had been in the bookstore for ten minutes. He knew he had no more time for caution. "We go on three," he said. He saw the women

88

jostling and preparing themselves, getting up onto their haunches and bracing themselves.

"One."

Glenda hefted the AR-15 and got slowly to her feet. She settled the weapon into her shoulder and curled her finger around the trigger. Made sure the safety was off and ready to fire.

"Two."

The rest of the women got to their feet, huddled in a tight knot. Their faces were racked with fear and tension. Cutter took a final glance along the street. The smoke from the burning dress shop was hanging low across the road in a black boiling haze. But through it, he thought he saw a sudden flicker of movement. He felt a dark lurch of icy fear...

"Three!" Glenda said with a sudden loud impulsive shout. She flung herself over the trolley, landing on her feet and slamming her shoulder against the frame of the doorway. She swept the weapon in a quick arc, and then started to run, the gun jumping and jostling as she tried to keep it steady. Behind her the other women were moving, more reluctantly, their steps hesitant, but swept up in the instant that fear and terror were forced down deep enough to drive them forward. Cutter cried out a warning. He leaped to his feet and thrust the Glock out in front of him. He narrowed his eyes, his panic rising as he tried to look past the fleeing figures of the women.

He was sure he had seen something.

He felt a sudden sickening slide in his guts – but by then it was too late for anything other than running... and praying.

* * *

The nearest SUV was a cherry red Dodge
Durango, left abandoned a couple of rows back from
the intersection lights. Cutter ran towards it with
his arms pumping and with fear clutching icy tight
around his chest as though the hounds from Hell
were on his heels.

But they weren't.

They were coming from a bank on the corner of
the block – a dozen undead ghouls who had been
drawn to the heavy sound of running footsteps, and
suddenly came shambling into the bright daylight at
an angle to intercept Cutter and the women.

Glenda saw them at the same instant as Cutter.
They were still thirty yards from the Durango when
she went down onto one knee and raised the AR-15
to her shoulder. The other women ran past, gasping
and crying out in fear. Glenda fired half-a-dozen
rounds, and three of the undead fell to the ground.
One of them didn't get up.

She fired again, taking careful aim at a woman
who was moving faster than the others, her face
twisted into a terrifying demented howl of outrage.
The left side of her face had been torn away and
flaps of livid flesh hung from her cheek bone. One of
her eyes was dangling from its socket, swinging like
a pendulum as she lurched forward. When the
bullets smashed into her, the ghoul stayed on its
feet, staggering in a circle and thrashing at the air
with its bloody hands. The bullets slapped loudly
into lifeless flesh, so that she jerked and juddered.
Then Glenda fired another round that caught the
woman in the forehead. She went over backwards –

her head snapped back by the vicious impact of the bullet – and lay dead on the warm blacktop.

Cutter ran past Glenda towards the Durango. The girl with the mousy brown hair was tugging desperately at the rear passenger door handle. She turned to Cutter and her eyes were huge and filled with terror. "There's a body in the back!" she screamed.

Cutter slammed into the back of the vehicle and saw the reflection of an undead shamble fill the vehicle's rear window. He turned and fired instinctively, a cry of shock loud in his throat.

The zombie was close. It was a man in a business suit, its face streaked with blood. Its mouth was open, roaring and gnashing. It was close enough for Cutter to see the broken bloody stumps of its teeth and smell the rank fetid stench of its breath.

He felt the gun kick in his hand as the sound of the shot echoed loud in his ears. The zombie was just a few feet away. Cutter's shot tore the back of the ghoul's head off.

He turned back to the woman at the car door. "What?"

"There's a man, hunched over in the back seat!" she cried, on the edge of hysteria. She flung the door open – and at the same instant the body on the back seat began to move, rising and turning towards her. The ghoul had once been a young man. Now he was a hideously disfigured nightmare, risen from the dead. He was wearing a t-shirt that had been ripped to shreds. It hung from his frame in tatters, exposing dreadful gaping holes in his chest. His face was awash with fresh blood, and black tufts of fur clung to its chin. The zombie's eyes flashed red with evil rage. It clawed at the woman, its hooked fingers snagging in the front of her blouse, ripping buttons and tugging her into the vehicle. On the seat beside the zombie was the mutilated carcass of a rat. The rodent's throat had been ripped open and its blood spilled across the soft padded seat.

The woman shrieked. The ghoul pulled her off balance and she was heaved head-first into the SUV. Cutter saw her legs kick wildly and he reached out for her. One of her shoes fell off and then suddenly the interior of the Durango was filled with a bright red eruption of arterial blood. It sprayed across the windows and coated the interior with the sticky cloying stench of sudden death. Cutter saw the woman's body gripped in a sudden seizure, and then the life went out of her.

He reeled away. Jillian and the other woman were running towards the next SUV. Cutter went back behind the Durango and grabbed Glenda's shoulder with a grip that was fierce with his own terror.

"Come on!" he shouted. Glenda was still firing. Two more of the ghouls lay dead on the ground, but the rest were shambling closer like a relentless tide of hideous death. Over her shoulder, driven into moaning madness by the loud percussive sound of the AR-15, more of the undead were appearing on the sidewalk, closing in from both sides of the street.

Cutter raised the Glock at one of the ghouls behind them. It was a young girl, maybe just into her teens. She had long blonde hair that was stringy with dirt and gore. She was wearing a long dress, so that it looked to Cutter as though she was gliding across the ground. She was coming on slowly, her head tilted at an impossible angle so that her cheek touched her shoulder, and her eyes were vacant and mindless. She was about twenty feet away. Cutter lined up for the head shot, but his hands were shaking. He felt the gun waver, and he knew that if he fired he would waste a precious round. He spun away.

"Come on!" he dragged Glenda to her feet. "Run!"

Jillian and the other woman were already at the next SUV, scrambling around the hood and tugging at the driver's side doors. It was an old blue Subaru Forester. Cutter pushed Glenda ahead of him and turned in a quick circle.

The zombie girl was still the closest threat, shambling towards them slowly, but others were coming more quickly from behind her, and from other nearby buildings. The ghouls that had surged from the bank on the corner were a more pressing threat. Their numbers were swelling.

He turned and ran.

Glenda had reached the SUV. She had the AR-15 propped on the roof of the Forester, resting the barrel on one of the vehicle's roof racks. She fired three quick shots at one of the ghouls swarming towards them. It was a figure wearing shredded army fatigues and a helmet. The man's face was emaciated, as though the blood had been sucked from his body, leaving the tatters of its skin shriveled and dry as parchment. The man's nose was missing and its lips had been gnarled away so that its gums were exposed and its teeth were bared in a moaning, howling rictus.

Glenda put a round into the empty, darkened socket that had once been his eye, and the ghoul was flung backwards, its helmet spinning from its exploded head in a high lazy arc.

"I'm out!" Glenda shouted. She shouldered the semi-automatic and spun Jillian around. She thrust her hand into the black nylon bag and felt for a fresh magazine.

The last woman in the group was about the same age as Glenda. Maybe twenty-five. Maybe a little older. She had short black hair and a pretty face, perched on a long graceful neck. She flung open the Forester's passenger door and scrambled into the vehicle. Slammed her fist down on the door lock, and then turned in her seat to lock the door behind where she sat. She was crying out in fear and panic, screaming to Cutter and the others to hurry. One of the ghouls broke from the group and slammed its bloody mangled hands against the glass of the window. Inside the Forester, the sound was like a sudden explosion. The woman flinched away and covered her face.

Cutter raised the Glock and fired. His first shot missed. He fired again, reaching across the roof of the Forester until the pistol was just inches away from the monster's ravaged face. The bullet went through its brain and it fell slowly to the ground, dragging its clawing hands down the side of the car with a sound like fingernails on a blackboard.

Glenda had reloaded the AR-15. Cutter saw the empty magazine clatter to the ground at her feet. Then she had the weapon up to her shoulder and was firing again with deadly, controlled shots at a range so close it was impossible for her to miss.

Jillian threw herself in behind the wheel of the Forester. The keys were still jangling in the ignition. She pumped the gas pedal with her foot and then fired up the motor. The engine coughed, whirred – and then died. Jillian punched the steering wheel in desperate panic. She tried again – and this time the Forester burst into growling life, the engine revving madly, and the air around the car hazing with exhaust fumes.

She leaned out of the door and screamed at Glenda and Cutter.

"Get in!" she shouted. The Forester's engine was howling, revving hard. Glenda fired four more shots, and then pulled open the rear door. She turned to Cutter. "I'll cover you. Get in!"

Cutter shook his head. "You get in!" he said, his voice loud in the sudden silence.

Cutter didn't wait. He fired two more shots at ghouls, then spun around and snapped off a shot at the undead teenage girl. She went down in a tangled heap, and rolled towards the gutter.

Glenda threw herself in through the open door of the Forester. She scrambled across the seat and smashed the passenger-side window with the butt of the rifle. The glass shattered into a thousand tiny diamonds and sprayed across the road. She thrust the barrel through the opening and fired two more shots. The ghouls were just a few feet away. The sound of their moans grew louder until it became an endless undulating wail. The fetid stench of their bodies hung in the air.

"Come on!" It was Jillian. She slammed the driver's door shut and gunned the engine again. Slipped the transmission into drive and stomped her foot on the brake to hold the car.

But Cutter wasn't listening.

Near where the zombie girl lay, was an apartment block. It was an old three-story building with an elegant old world façade and heavy glass entry doors. From one of the top floor windows,

Cutter suddenly saw a movement and his eyes flicked to it, expecting fresh danger.

It was a white bath towel.

There was a fresh-faced teenage boy wearing a bulky padded jacket and a baseball cap. He was holding the towel out of the open window, the fabric rippling and undulating gently in the breeze. Written in large hasty lettering was the message *'We are Alive!'* and then next to it was the sign of the cross.

Cutter stared.

Beside the teenage boy, another figure suddenly appeared, framed against the darkened window. It was a middle-aged man. He was balding. He had a red fleshy face, and he was wearing some kind of a dark coat. The man cried out to Cutter.

"In God's name, please help us!"

Cutter paused. Time seemed to stand still. He turned back to the Forester. The open door was right beside him. The women were in the car. Glenda was firing again as the wave of ghouls pressed closer like a suffocating wall of death. Escape was right there – waiting for him. He had done it. He had led the women out onto the horror-filled road and they had made it to a vehicle. He had survived.

He glanced beyond the roof of the Forester. Time was up. The ghouls were at the passenger-side doors. He could see Glenda firing, and the undead were so close that the shaft of gun flame joined the muzzle of the AR-15 and a zombie's head, hurling it backwards like a bundle of rags to the ground.

Cutter decided.

He slammed the door shut and punched on the roof of the Forester. Jillian's face twisted towards him, pressed against the glass, her mouth open in terror.

"Go!" Cutter shouted. "Head for the suburbs!"

Jillian's eyes became enormous. She was shouting at him, but Cutter wasn't listening. Then he felt something crash against his waist and he reeled in sudden fright. It was Glenda. She was shoving at the rear door with her feet, trying to kick it back open. She was shouting to him in fear and desperation. Cutter turned and bent at the waist. He shook his head. Glenda stared at him aghast. She was crying. He could see the anguish and tormented terror in her eyes.

Cutter nodded slowly. "It's okay," he said, mouthing the words because he knew she couldn't hear him above the wail of the ghouls. "It's okay. This is what I want."

Then he smiled.

Glenda slumped back against the seat, cold with shock – numb and staring vacantly. Then Jillian took her foot off the brake and the Forester roared away from the clamoring clawing hands of the zombies, lurching dangerously at the intersection and then turning right towards open road in a blue cloud of smoke and burning rubber.

Cutter turned away from the ghouls.

And ran.

* * *

The heavy glass entry doors to the apartment block were twenty feet away. Cutter leaped over the body of the dead zombie girl and slammed his fists against them. They didn't budge. The glass was darkly tinted and he pressed his face against it. The doors had been barricaded with jumbled furniture.

He turned and glanced over his shoulder. The ghouls were swarming across the street, and more were shambling along the sidewalk towards him, teetering and unsteady, but remorseless. He stepped back towards the gutter and looked up urgently.

"The fire escape!" that man in the dark coat was shouting down at him, crying out, his voice hoarse. Cutter looked left. There was a narrow alleyway beside the building, choked with large steel dumpsters filled with rotting trash. "Down the alley!" the man flailed his arms.

Cutter clenched his jaw and tucked the pistol down the front of his jeans. The figure of a ghoul appeared suddenly to his right. It was a woman. In life she might have been quite beautiful. In death she was a shrieking, howling nightmare. She was wearing a blouse and skirt, and as she drew within just a few feet of where Cutter stood, her body began to writhe and undulate. Her arms came up, her fingers splayed into claws, and her eyes snapped wide and red through long brown tangles of hair that hung down over her face. The woman had been bitten on her shoulders and arms. Cutter could see the horrendous savagery of the wounds, still oozing in thick brown gore. Around each gash, her skin was covered with angry puss-filled sores. The woman took a shambling step closer and then suddenly vomited bloody gore that heaved from somewhere deep within her guts and gushed down over her chin and throat.

Cutter shifted so that his weight was on his right foot, ready to kick out. The ghoul pressed forward.

Cutter waited, knowing he had only seconds to spare. All around him the undead closed in, reaching for him, howling and hissing at him. He glanced past the undead woman's shape and guessed it was fifteen feet to the alleyway. He could still make it.

And then suddenly he felt an icy claw wrap around his ankle. He looked down in horror. The zombie girl stared up at him, its lips drawn back in an inhuman wail of triumph and its tongue flicking hungrily, as though already anticipating the taste of him. Cutter could see the lethal malevolence in the zombie's eyes, and he felt himself shudder. The girl was leaking brown gore from the side of her face where Cutter's bullet had ripped away part of her cheek. Suddenly the air exploded with the sound of the undead girl's triumphant scream.

Cutter went cold with dread. He moved instinctively, jamming the heel of his boot down hard on the girl's arm and heard brittle bones break. The undead girl hissed and rose to her knees. Her other bloody hand clawed at his jeans.

Cutter snatched at the pistol and fired three shots into the zombie girl's head. The skull collapsed, and the body was flung backwards.

Without hesitating, Cutter turned and fired twice more at the woman in front of him. Her head snapped back against its neck and then it dropped to its knees and fell sideways to the sidewalk. Cutter leaped over her and ran for the alley.

He reached the dumpsters and stole a final look over his shoulder. The horde of ghouls was like a solid wall before him. He saw some of them teetering and swaying. He saw others knocked aside – and then from the back of the group came a man dressed in an immaculate dark suite, wearing a blue tie and a crisp white shirt. He was running, his gait awkward and uncoordinated, but cleaving a swathe through the undead horde, heading directly for Cutter. He burst through the front rank of the group and came at a run. Cutter hesitated. The man looked.... like a man.

He raised the pistol slowly. The man's mouth snapped open. Cutter took his finger off the trigger and paused in an instant of numb confusion.

And then the man roared in rage and its eyes blazed with infected fury. Cutter flung up the pistol and snapped off a shot. The bullet struck the man in the forehead, punching a hole between his eyes. He stopped – spun round in a circle – and Cutter saw the terrible gouged wounds that had been ripped into the man's back, exposing his spine and organs. The zombie collapsed to the ground. Cutter aimed and fired again, and heard the hollow 'click' of an empty magazine.

"Shit!" Cutter swore. He jammed the useless pistol into the waistband of his jeans and scrambled up the side of a dumpster and over the piles of rotting refuse.

* * *

Beyond the dumpsters was more garbage, stacked against the brick wall of the apartment block. Cutter dropped to the ground and swept the alley cautiously.

The wall of the building opposite was covered in colorful graffiti painted around the dark shapes of two doors. They were brown timber things with bolts and padlocks on them. Cutter kicked aside black trash bags and scrambled over an old sofa, its fabric worn and faded. The dark shape of a rat scurried out from under a bag of rotting garbage and Cutter stomped down hard on the rodent. It squealed its agony – a sound like a newborn baby in pain – until he crushed it into mush beneath the heel of his boot.

The alley was about forty feet long and he followed the wall of the building to the end and glanced around the corner. There was a fire escape in front of him. He looked up. He could see the boy. The bottom extension of the ladder dropped down and Cutter began to climb. He was trembling, his body still filled with surging adrenalin and fear.

But he had made it.

He had leaped from the frying pan – back into the fire.

* * *

Cutter waited while the boy wordlessly hunched to retract the extension steps of the fire escape, and then followed as he was led onto the top landing and then into a dim passageway.

Cutter's stood still for a moment and let his eyes adjust to the gloom. The passageway ran from right to left, and at each end was a dark door. There was another door opposite him. It was a heavy timber piece with three shiny brass locks. The boy was ahead of him. He knocked on the door it was flung open by the man Cutter had seen at the window. He had a gun in his hand and a fraught, fearful expression on his face. The boy brushed past him and disappeared into the apartment beyond, leaving Cutter face-to-face with the man.

From the window, Cutter had guessed the man to be middle-aged, but now they were facing each other across the short width of the passageway, he changed that assessment. The man was probably in his mid-forties. He had big fleshy features: a huge bulbous nose and heavy jowls. His mouth was wide, drawn into a grim line, but his eyes were bright and sparkling, as though lit by some kind of secret joy. He was short and broad – and carrying most of his weight around an ample fleshy stomach.

"Bless you, Samaritan," the man said. The gun went into his pocket and his arm went out to Cutter. Cutter shook hands with the man and let himself be drawn into the apartment. He heard the door close and the 'snick' of security locks behind his back while he stood and studied his new surroundings.

He was standing in a small living room that opened to a kitchen. Beyond the kitchen Cutter saw a short hallway with a polished board floor. There were three doors: bathroom and a couple of bedrooms he guessed. That was all. It was tiny. The place smelled of smoke and stale coffee. He could see a clutter of dishes in the sink, and a dozen candles of assorted shapes and colors on the kitchen bench. Nearby where he stood was a three-seat sofa that had seen better days and a new flat-screen television. There was a lamp, a coffee-table, and not much else. The window opposite was wide open and sunlight and sound streamed into the room. Cutter went and leaned against the sill. Looked down.

There was about a hundred undead zombies gathered around the front doors of the apartment building, moaning and wailing, but without the frenzied edge to the sound that he had heard when they were attacking him. His eyes drifted to the entrance of the alleyway where another group of undead were milling around the heavy steel dumpsters. Cutter turned quickly to the man.

"Are the doors downstairs going to hold?"

The man nodded. "They're solid enough," he said. "And the things can't climb. We're safe."

"What about the rest of the apartments? There are three stories. Have you barricaded the stairs? The place could be full – "

The man shook his head. "It's clear," He said. "There's only us and Mr. Walker in 3B. The rest of the building is vacant. Has been for the last month. The owners are re-developing."

Cutter stopped. His body was still pumped full of adrenalin and fear, so that his mind raced, looking for threats and danger. "What about this Walker guy? Have you seen him?"

The man nodded. "Just a few minutes ago, down on the street. He was the ghoul in the business suit you just shot."

Cutter nodded, then paused. He held out his hand again. "My name is Jack Cutter."

The man crossed the room and took Cutter's hand in a double-fisted grip. "I'm Robert Davidson," he said. "But everyone calls me Father Bob."

Cutter felt a sudden jolt. "You're a priest?"

"A pastor," the man said and shrugged. "But in these troubled times, son, you can call me anything you want. Priest – pastor … I'm a man of God, regardless of your faith."

Cutter felt a creeping cold numbness. He stared into the man's twinkling eyes for long silent seconds trying to make sense of the sudden turmoil of his emotions. Cutter wasn't a superstitious man, but somewhere in the dark distant recesses of his mind he felt fate's ironic touch. He shook his head. Everything had altered in an instant.

"Are you okay, son?" Father Bob asked.

Cutter backed away. Nodded curtly. But he wasn't okay. He turned and looked around the room again, then realized the television screen was black and blank. "Is the power off?"

The pastor nodded. "Just a few minutes ago. Just after Sam saw you on the street."

Cutter nodded. His mind reeled, distracted and confused. He frowned, trying to force himself to think in the moment. "Do you have supplies? Do you have plenty of water and food?"

Father Bob nodded. "We have canned food to last a week if we're careful, and we filled the bathtub with water yesterday. We have candles – and I have this gun."

He fetched the pistol from his pocket and held it up to show Cutter. "I have plenty of ammunition too."

It was a revolver. It had Smith & Wesson stamped on the short stainless steel barrel. "It's a 44 Magnum," the pastor said. He held the weapon out to Cutter but he shook his head.

"You're a pastor – and you have a gun?"

Father Bob smiled wryly. "You know what they say," his voice suddenly took on a broad southern accent, "A bible in one hand, and a gun in the other..."

Cutter pulled the Glock from his jeans and held it out. "Do you have ammunition for this? It's empty."

Father Bob shook his head with slow regret but then made a sudden curious face. "I don't," he said. "But Walker might. We could raid his apartment. He's bound to have food and supplies – and he might have a gun."

Cutter nodded. He was trying to think the situation through, looking for dangers. He frowned and thought back to the bunker below the bookstore.

What would Hos do?

Suddenly the silence was pierced by a series of shrill and terrified screams. Cutter spun back to the window and leaned out.

A group of people suddenly burst from the shade of the sidewalk, out into the bright sunlight. They were running in terror, scattering in all directions. Cutter recognized the lumbering shape of John Grainger and several of the women. He swore bitterly.

"Get to the cars!" he shouted, his voice indignant with futile rage. "This way! Run towards the intersection!"

It was no use. They had been driven from the bookstore's bunker by the sudden darkness, and they ran in scrambling terror. Some fled across the street, dodging between abandoned burning cars and disappeared into the buildings on the opposite side of the street. Others ran east and Cutter lost sight of them. Grainger and three of the women ran blindly out into the middle of the road and spun around as though disoriented. Cutter saw one of the women trip and fall to her knees. She cried out in pain and panic, but the others had run past her, weaving and jinking as though lost in a giant maze.

The zombies came for them. The undead spilled from the buildings, and the swarm of dark undead shapes clustered around the apartment block's doors below suddenly turned and began to hunt the fleeing survivors.

Cutter could only watch helplessly. He felt the press of Father Bob's bulky shape in the window frame beside him.

"Do you know them?"

Cutter nodded. "I was trapped with them last night in the bookshop."

On the street below, John Grainger had been cornered against the side of a yellow cab. He threw his hands up to shield his face and screamed once in terror. The zombies pressed around him and flailed with bloody arms. Grainger sank out of sight, and the zombies set about tearing his body to shreds.

One of the other women turned and ran in screaming horror. She fled towards the sidewalk. She could sense the zombies closing from every side, and when she turned to glance over her shoulder, she ran head-first into a plate glass shop front window, slicing her body to pieces and killing her in an instant gush of blood. Cutter looked away. The screams lingered for just a few more minutes, growing fainter – becoming weaker – until finally no one was screaming because no one was left alive.

Cutter took a deep breath and closed his eyes. He could feel the room reeling like the whole world was tilting off its axis.

When he opened his eyes again, Father Bob was clutching at a bible, muttering a soft silent prayer.

"You have to get out of here," Cutter said. "You can't stay in the city. Sooner or later you'll run out of supplies. Sooner or later you're going to be faced with the choice of starving to death, or trying to escape."

106

Father Bob nodded heavily. "I know," he said. "That's why you've come. You're the answer to my prayers, son. We need your help to reach safety. Sam and I won't make it on our own. I know that."

Cutter began to shake his head in protest but at the same instant he heard a door close. He turned towards the sound – and saw a young woman standing in the hallway. She was maybe nineteen or twenty years old with soft blonde hair, wearing denim jeans and a blue sweatshirt with the name of a college football team written in large letters across where her breasts swelled beneath the fabric. She had honey-colored skin and vivid blue eyes. She was holding the bulky padded jacket in one hand and the baseball cap in the other.

Cutter stood stunned for long moments, until finally Father Bob put his arm paternally around the woman's shoulder, smiling fondly.

"Mr. Cutter, this is my daughter, Samantha. You two have already met."

The woman held out her hand demurely and Cutter felt the warm softness of her skin. She smiled and her teeth were perfect and white, and her voice a shy breathy whisper.

"Hello," she said. "Sorry I didn't think to introduce myself on the fire escape landing."

* * *

Without the disguise of the bulky jacket and cap, the girl was slim and lithe, with long, almost coltish, legs. Cutter watched her from the sofa as she brought him an opened can of cold beans and a spoon.

"Are you sure you don't want a plate?"

Cutter shook his head. He suddenly remembered how hungry he was. He hadn't eaten in almost twenty-four hours.

The girl wrung her hands apologetically. "It's not much. I'm sorry..."

Cutter smiled and attacked the food with relish. "It's great," he said. "I appreciate it." The girl went back to the kitchen and returned with a plastic bottle of water. She set it down wordlessly and then went to stand by her father at the open window.

Cutter finished eating quickly. He drank half the bottle of water and sat back for a moment, overcome by the sudden realization that this fleeting moment of food, drink and comfort were now considered life's luxuries. He looked up at the pastor and fought of a sudden wave of weary drowsiness.

"Why are you still here?" he asked. "Why are you here at all? Don't priests have congregations? Shouldn't you be somewhere out in the suburbs, tending to a flock?"

Father Bob sighed heavily. He pushed himself away from the window and stood in the middle of the room, seeming to fill the space. His expression was suddenly bleak.

"I do have a flock," he nodded. "In a little town a ways south of here called Granton. Good town. Pretty. And good people too," he smiled fondly recalling some distant memory. "But Samantha and I moved here to Newbridge for a reason..."

"What reason?"

"Cancer," Father Bob said and forced a humorless smile. "I've got cancer. So I took leave from the church and came here two months ago because it's close to the hospital. It's why we're in this little apartment. And it's why I prayed to God that a man like you would come to our aid."

Cutter sat blankly. "Curable?"

Father Bob shook his head with heavy regret. "No, son."

There was a long silence. Finally Cutter asked softly. "How long have you got?"

Father Bob shrugged. "I'm already on borrowed time," he said. "It could be any day." His complexion turned suddenly to ash, and the sparkle in the man's eye faded.

His daughter came to him then, her expression heartbreakingly tender. She hugged herself to him and Cutter saw the shine of unshed tears in her eyes.

The big man pulled her close to him. He kissed her forehead, and they stood in absolute silence for long seconds as though drawing emotional strength from each other.

Finally Father Bob broke from the embrace and stared Cutter hard in the eye. "That's why I need you," he said bluntly. "I need you to get my baby girl to safety. I need you to promise me that if I fall, you'll get her somewhere away from here."

Cutter stared at the man for long seconds. He felt that same sense of premonition and fate that he had first felt when he had found out the man was a pastor. Finally he nodded slowly.

"I'll do it," Cutter agreed. "But I have a price."

Father Bob's expression became suddenly guarded. His gaze turned to ice. He drew Samantha close to him again, holding her to him protectively.

"Name it," he said, the words edged with wary caution.

Cutter's eyes flicked from the pastor's expression to the face of his daughter. She was staring back at him, holding his gaze with her chin tilted in a gesture of resilience and defiance. She was quite beautiful, he realized.

"I want you to hear my confession," Cutter said.

* * *

Father Bob stood perfectly still for long moments, staring at Cutter and seeing, for the first time, an urgency and desperation in the tall stranger's face. The pastor shook his head slowly. "Son, I'm a pastor – not a Catholic priest. I don't take confessions." He paused and thought about his next words before beginning to talk again, as though suddenly he was back in his little church delivering a Sunday sermon.

"These are dark days," Father Bob said. "It's normal for people to find faith and God when the world seems on the brink of disaster. It's normal for men to question everything they once believed in and look to the Almighty as their Savior. What you're feeling now is exactly what millions of other lost souls are feeling. Afraid. You're terrified that life on earth is over. You want to save your soul. Sadly, it's too often been moments like this in mankind's history that people look to God and eternal life as a desperate source of comfort."

Cutter shook his head with irritation. He stood up. "I'm not Catholic," he said bluntly. "In fact I've only been to church twice in my whole life. Once was when I got married. The second time was a week ago when I stood over the coffins of my dead wife and young son."

More silence. The two men stared at each other, the girl suddenly forgotten. "And I'm not some religious zealot suddenly converted to the faith because I'm surrounded by death," Cutter persisted. "This has nothing to do with the world going to hell," he snapped. He sensed his anger rising and he forced himself to take a deep calming breath.

"You said you were a man of God. Well I've been talking to God a lot over these last few days, and he's not answering," Cutter said. "I've never prayed before in my life, but over the last week it seems like all I've been doing. I keep asking him why I'm still alive and my wife and son are cold and buried in the ground. I need answers, dammit. Maybe he will hear me through you."

Father Bob began to nod his head with slow understanding.

"You called me a Samaritan when we first met," Cutter went on. Then shook his head bitterly. "Well I'm not," he said. "I'm not a Samaritan at all. I didn't come to help you because it was the right thing to do. I came to help you to give God another chance to kill me," he admitted. "I did it yesterday, out on the street too. I tried to save a man – but not to help him. I tried to get him to safety when I knew it was impossible... because I wanted to give God the chance to kill me, like he killed my wife and child. And that's what I did again today," Cutter's voice began to rise with his anguished pain. "That's what brought me here to you. That's why I risked my life – not because of any noble or Christian gesture. I'm not that good a man. I did it because I wanted to know whether I'm supposed to be alive at all." He turned away suddenly. He could feel the sudden sting of tears in his eyes.

Father Bob's voice suddenly became gentle and compassionate. "Would you like to tell me what happened?"

Cutter nodded. "That's what I want," he said. "That's my price for taking you and your daughter to safety. I want to know why God let me live, when I'm the one who is responsible for the death of my wife and boy."

* * *

Cutter and Father Bob left Samantha standing in the doorway of the apartment armed with the revolver, and strode down the darkened passage.

"I don't suppose you have keys?" Cutter asked when they were out front of 3B.

Father Bob shook his head.

Cutter shrugged. He backed up and took three paces towards the door then lashed out hard with a sidekick aimed an inch below the worn brass lock. The timber door splintered, but the frame was metal. Cutter felt the impact jar through his boot and all the way up his leg. He kicked again. The door began to sag. The timber around the lock fragmented. On the third kick, the timber finally gave way and the heavy door slammed back against its hinges.

The two men stood in doorway and stared into the gloomy opening.

"Mr. Walker was a lawyer," Father Bob explained for no apparent reason. Cutter frowned.

"And he was living in a little up-town apartment?" It made no sense. His eyes swept around the interior. The layout was a mirror image of the pastor's tiny unit.

"A divorced lawyer," Father Bob added, and then glanced at Cutter as though that explained it all.

They went in cautiously. There were rats in the kitchen. The refrigerator door had been left open and the thick stench of rotting food filled the air. Dark scurrying shapes skittered away into deeper shadows. Cutter's eyes swept the room quickly. There were cockroaches in the sink, feasting on food scraps and the floor was sticky with spoiled food the rodents had dragged from the refrigerator. He checked the cupboards and found a dozen cans of soup and packets of instant noodles – but not much else.

He went back into the tiny living room.

Father Bob was rummaging through a chest of drawers.

"Anything?" Cutter asked.

The pastor shook his head. Cutter nodded. "I'll check the bedrooms and bathroom."

The first bedroom was empty. No furniture, no bed. Just a small curtained window in the wall opposite and faded, peeling wallpaper that was brown with water stains. The second bedroom had an unmade double bed, a wardrobe and a narrow set of bedside drawers. The air was musty and damp. Cutter found a dozen expensive suits and just as many silk shirts in the wardrobe. He also found a stack of old tattered porn magazines.

The bed was unmade. Cutter lifted the mattress but found nothing. In the small set of drawers he found reams of paperwork, a couple of packets of cigarettes and a lighter. He put the lighter into his pocket.

The bathroom was just a narrow cubicle large enough for a bathtub and a small washbasin. On the wall above the sink was a slim mirror-fronted medicine cabinet. There were dirty unwashed clothes on the floor and a damp discarded towel. Cutter went to the sink and looked inside the cabinet. There was the usual collection of medicines, a couple of bottles of expensive cologne – and a gun. Beside the gun was a box of ammunition.

Cutter reached for the weapon. It was another Glock, similar to the one he had taken from Hos's dead body. He stuffed the weapon inside the waistband of his jeans and snatched at the box of ammunition.

When he came back into the tiny living area, he found Father Bob sitting on a straight-backed chair. He was reading.

"What did you find?" Cutter asked.

Father Bob held up the book. "The Koran," he said with a look of puzzled surprise on his face. "It appears our Mr. Walker was a Muslim."

Cutter shrugged. "So?"

Father Bob made a face. "So nothing," he said defensively. "It's just something about the man I never knew." Then he noticed the box in Cutters hand. "Ammunition?"

Cutter nodded. "And a gun."

Father Bob heaved himself wearily from the chair. He looked past Cutter's shoulder, back into the kitchen. "What about the food you found?"

"We take it," Cutter said. "We take it all."

* * *

The night fell like a heavy shroud, hunting away the last flaming rays of sunset and plunging the world around them into a place of darkness and dangerous shadows.

Cutter stood by the window and stared. The city street was dark now. The fires had burned themselves out during the afternoon, and a stiffening breeze had swept the smoke into a hazy scar on the horizon.

Now the street below was silent.

The zombies had drifted away from the apartment doors, shuffling into the night, and the only light was from the first stars and a thin slice of moon that rose behind the high buildings on the opposite side of the deserted street.

Samantha and her father came into the room from the kitchen carrying three plates and bottles of water. Father Bob muttered a brief prayer of thanks, and then they sat together on the lumpy sofa eating canned ham and three-day-old bread.

Candles burned, filling the room with soft flickering light, and Cutter watched the shadows leap and play on the wall opposite, his mind drifting, his body leaden and weary.

He felt wrung out: as though the tension and stress had burned through the last reserves of his energy. He felt his eyes getting heavy and it took a defiant act of will for him to resist the urge to slump over and sleep.

He dragged his hands across his face and blinked his eyes wide. "We had a deal..." he said to Father Bob.

The pastor nodded gravely. He handed his plate to Samantha. "Take these into the kitchen please, honey. And then I want you to do an hour of bible study in your room. I need to talk to Mr. Cutter, and it's a conversation we need to have in private."

Samantha's eyes flicked from her father's face to Cutter's, and a shadow passed behind her eyes. But she stood obediently and left the room without a word.

Father Bob sighed. "It's been hard on her," he said sadly. "She lost her mother just a year ago. And then a month later I found out I had cancer. She's a good girl – but she's a pastor's daughter – and that means she's not prepared for what the world has become. If anyone can be prepared..."

Cutter said nothing for a long moment. The girl had the flare of hip and breast of a fully-grown woman. It was only in her face that he had seen the suggestion of naïve innocence. "How old is she?"

"Twenty," the pastor said. "She'll turn twenty-one next month." He sighed heavily. "Sometimes I wonder if it's the one thing that has kept me alive," he confessed. "I promised her I'd be there for her birthday..."

Cutter slumped back in the sofa and sighed. He thought about what the world was becoming and the realization made his despair even darker. Once, a man like him could dream of a future, and of a family, and of watching his son grow up. And once a man like Father Bob could dream of his daughter's birthday and plan for her future.

Once – but not now.

Now there was no future. Plans were pointless. Life was too temporary. Then he realized it had always been that way – fate had always shattered futures.

But what was happening to the world now was something very different. It was brutal and ruthless and merciless... and inhuman.

All a man had now was the very next moment, because beyond that was only uncertainty and peril.

Cutter closed his eyes. He felt the waves of drowsiness beating at him, dragging him towards sleep. He felt himself beginning to drift, and he jolted upright in the sofa.

Father Bob was watching him.

"Do you still want to talk?"

Cutter nodded. He got to his feet. He went to the window and stared down at the street for long moments, then turned back to where the pastor was sitting. In the flickering weak light of the candles, Cutter's face was shrouded in shadow, and he stood like that, gathering his thoughts until the words simply began to spill from him and he could not stop them.

"My wife – Christina – she was a good woman," Cutter said, his voice faltering. "We had been high-school sweethearts, and when we married we bought a little farm out west of here. We were happy. We were in love, and then when we found out she was pregnant, life just seemed to get better."

Cutter started to pace the room, keeping in the shadows. He felt his hands bunch into tight fists and the tension began to rise up through his back and shoulders. "When my son Scotty was born, we left the farm and moved closer to Newbridge," Cutter said softly. "He was ill as a baby, and we needed to

117

be closer to town, but as he started to grow, he got stronger. I had been a farmer, just like my father before me. But now we were living in the suburbs and I needed a new profession. So I started painting," he shrugged. "Don't ask me why – I just don't know how it happened. Christina thought I had some talent so I stuck at it. Eventually I broke into some commercial galleries, and then a publisher in New York asked me to design a cover for one of their authors."

Cutter stood against the far wall, his eyes unfocussed, and behind his blank gaze his mind was imagining a time and place beyond the tiny little apartment.

"I did well. Things were perfect. Christina started studying law, and Scotty turned six. I was living the dream," Cutter said, but there was bitter anguish in his voice now. "Until last Sunday when we came into Newbridge…"

Cutter stopped talking, and Father Bob let the silence hang in the empty space between them. He watched the tall dark stranger move restlessly in the shadows and he felt the man's despair.

"Did something happen?"

Cutter nodded. "Yeah," he said harshly. "Yeah, something happened on the road into the city."

"What, son? Tell me what happened?"

Cutter looked up. There were tears in his eyes and he shook his head sorrowfully. "We were in Christina's beat-up old Ford," Cutter began, but now there was a wavering tremble in his voice. A heartbroken sound of regret. "I was driving. Scotty was in the back seat. We had just bought him his first baseball mitt…" his voice drifted wanly for a moment then came back stronger. "I was driving a little too fast. We were getting closer to the city. I leaned over to change the music on the radio – and somehow missed a set of traffic lights," Cutter said. There was another long moment of dead silence, and then his voice somehow became blank and devoid of all emotion. "We went through a red light. A truck was coming out from the intersection. It was already into the intersection when we drove through. The car slammed into the side of the truck. I saw it too late. I tried to brake and swerve, but all I did was turn the car sideways. Christina and Scotty were crushed to death. The side of the car folded in. The impact killed them instantly. Somehow I survived. Untouched."

Cutter sagged, as though the telling of the tragedy had somehow left him deflated and broken. He stood, silent in the shadows and cuffed brusquely at his eyes.

Cutter saw Father Bob nod, and then reach for his battered bible. He held the book in his hand as he spoke, and his voice was deep and resonate.

"Son, sometimes we wonder why God does the things he does. And sometimes we wonder why life can be so cruel. We ask ourselves why would a compassionate God take the innocent and the ones we cherish and leave us – the unworthy – here to suffer," the pastor said solemnly. "There are different reasons for us all, but for you, the reason is clear. Your wife and son died before this holocaust. They died living life to the fullest, never knowing fear of terror. Be grateful for that. They were released into His arms before the horror. That's a blessing."

Cutter said nothing. He stood as a darker shape amongst the shadows, silent and unmoving.

"And you have been spared because your task is not complete," Father Bob went on. "He needs you. He has work for you in these troubled times. That's why He saved you, and that's why He sent you to Samantha and me. You can call it coincidence, or you can call it fate. Either way, God led you to this place at this time for just one reason. Because your work is here... with us."

* * *

Samantha came from the hallway holding a candle in front of her, the soft golden glow lighting her face and hair so that she appeared almost angelic.

She sat quietly on the sofa beside her father, and Cutter came from the shadows. He dropped to his haunches before them both.

"We need to leave here in the morning," he said, watching their eyes carefully. "We can't wait for the zombies to drift away from the city. There could be other pockets of people like us in a hundred buildings like this. That's going to be enough to keep them interested – and lingering. Our only hope is to get to a place that is less populated. It's our best chance of survival."

Samantha stared into his eyes. "You're coming with us, Mr. Cutter?"

He nodded. "I am," he said.

Samantha said nothing. She glanced at her father and her expression was serious as she seemed to look an unspoken question. Father Bob took her hand in his and nodded.

"How do you propose we get away from the city?" Samantha asked him. Her tone was level, and Cutter had the bizarre feeling that he was being interviewed for a job.

"We find a car," he said. "Preferably a SUV. If not, something sturdy that will take a beating."

"Just like that?" Samantha asked.

"Pretty much," Cutter said, and then realized it wasn't enough. He sighed. "Last night I was trapped in the bookstore with a group of women and a couple of other men. You saw us when we made our break this morning. We lost a woman, but the other three escaped. You saw it. I figure the same kind of plan will work again." He got to his feet and strode to the window. He looked down. The night was black. "When daylight comes, we'll pick a vehicle and go for it," he said. "We have the advantage of height here. That means we'll have some kind of warning – or at least some idea of what the undead are doing before we break for the street."

He went back towards the sofa. "If we need to we can create some kind of distraction. It might buy us enough time."

Father Bob nodded his head, but he knew it would not be as easy as Cutter was making the plan sound.

But it was a plan, and he noticed how the man's voice suddenly had become resolute and determined. He sensed Cutter was rising to the challenge.

"Where will we go?" the pastor asked. "What was the plan you had when you escaped with the other women?"

Cutter shook his head. "I didn't have a plan then," he confessed. "Once we made it to a car, we were just going to get out of the city."

"And go where?" Samantha asked.

Cutter shook his head again. "I didn't know, then."

"But you do now?"

Cutter smiled. "Yeah," he said. "Now I know." He reached into his pocket and found the wallet he had taken from Hos's dead body. He pulled out the man's driver's license and held it up to the candle-light.

"This man was killed," Cutter said. "He was with us in the bookstore. He was a survivalist. He told me he had been preparing for a disaster situation like this for years. He told me he had a compound —a remote property away from the city that had a generator, six months of food and water, and a supply of weapons," Cutter explained. "That's where we are going."

He looked at the license and read the address, and there was another eerie moment of fate as he said softly:

"He lived at 34 Eden Gardens, Guthrie." Cutter looked at the pastor and then to Samantha. There was the faintest hint of an ironic smile at the corner of his lip. "The garden of Eden..." he said.

Cutter knew the area. Guthrie was a rural community about forty miles north-east of Newbridge. He had a vague childhood recollection of rolling fields and leafy tree-lined roads with clustered mailboxes, and dirt trails that led to remote farmhouses.

Father Bob glanced from Cutter's face towards the ceiling and muttered another heart-felt prayer of thanks.

Four.
Escape.

They were up at sunrise.

Cutter awoke in an awkward tangle of limbs, curled up on the sofa. He had dragged the three-seater across the door as a barricade and had slept fitfully. Now, as he stared at the living room ceiling, he felt the grip of seized muscles he never knew existed.

He got up and stretched. Dragged the sofa away from the apartment door. Then he heard noise in the kitchen.

Samantha was standing at the sink wearing a long t-shirt that covered the tops of her legs – and nothing else. Cutter could clearly see the perky shape of her breasts under the thin material as she turned to him, and morning light through the narrow window behind her cast the shadow of her thighs in tantalizing silhouette. Her hair was a messy, sleepy tumble and she smiled at him shyly.

"Sorry," she said. "I didn't mean to wake you." She pushed at her hair self consciously. "I was just getting organized."

There was a big canvas carry bag on the kitchen counter, and an assortment of canned food beside it. Cutter nodded. "Don't forget a can opener," he said.

Samantha smiled. "It's already packed."

Cutter stepped closer and looked inside the bag. Samantha stood beside him, watching his face as he applied himself to the challenge of deciding what supplies to take, and what must be left behind.

"We'll need water," Cutter said. "Lots of it."

Samantha nodded. "I have bottles ready," she said. "I thought I'd pack the soup first because it's condensed. "One can will make a meal for all three of us."

Cutter thought for a moment. The logic made sense. "Good idea," he said. "But remember one of us has to carry this bag, plus we'll have weapons. So weight is important."

She leaned across the kitchen counter, and for one brief second her shoulder brushed his, and he saw a glimpse of the soft pale flesh of her breast through a gape in the fabric of her nightie. Samantha picked up a can of stewed beef and another one of spaghetti. "Do you have any preferences?"

Cutter shook his head. He heard footsteps behind him and turned to see Father Bob standing in the open doorway. The man looked sick. His face was ashen, his features somehow blurred and worn down. Behind the strained smile, Cutter saw agonizing pain in the man's expression.

Cutter said nothing.

"Good morning," Father Bob muttered. He unscrewed the top off a plastic bottle of water and swallowed a handful of assorted tablets.

Samantha went to her father and hugged him. The big man wrapped an arm around her shoulder and stared over the top of her head directly at Cutter.

"We must go soon," he silently mouthed the words. Cutter understood. He nodded.

* * *

124

Father Bob and Cutter leaned out through the apartment's living room window and stared at the street below. The big man sighed heavily. "How do we do this?"

The area looked like a battlefield. The wrecked and burned out cars down on the road were now just charred blackened shells, strewn across every lane of traffic, amongst dozens of other dead abandoned vehicles. The road was streaked with oil and blood.

The sky was clear and blue, the buildings across the street casting long shadows. Smoke still drifted lazily from the shop fronts that had burned through the night, and glass littered the blacktop.

The corpse of the zombie in the business suit Cutter had shot through the head was still laying stretched out on the blacktop near one of the dumpsters. During the night vermin had mutilated the body. There were other undead still lying in the street, and the stench rose on the air until it became a black oily taste in the back of Cutter's throat.

He saw the new red SUV he had led the women towards just twenty-four hours earlier. He pointed.

"The red Durango," he said. "That was the car I was trying for yesterday," he explained. "See how it's been left just a few rows back from the lights?"

The pastor nodded, and Cutter went on quickly. "It's on this side of the street, and there is a clear run if we can get past the pick-up in front of it." He drew a route in the air with his finger. "If we can get up onto the sidewalk and past that set of bench seats on the other side of the alley, we can make it round the corner and escape."

The pastor frowned. "But... yesterday..."

Cutter nodded. "When we got the doors open there was a zombie on the back seat eating a rat. The zombie dragged one of the women I was with into the car. I couldn't save her..."

"They could still be there. In the car."

Cutter nodded again. "They could be – but we'll have to take the chance. There's nothing else down on the road that isn't blocked by too much traffic to be useful."

The pastor pointed to a blue pick up that was about a dozen rows back from the lights. It had big off-road tires and a solid nudge bar welded in front of the grille. "What about that one?"

Cutter shook his head. The truck was east of the building. That meant running back towards the bookstore. "We would be running right into them," Cutter said. "And I don't see how we could reach the lights. Even with the nudge bar, we're going to be moving too slowly, and making a hell of a lot of noise. The zombies would be swarming all over us."

Father Bob looked back down at the Durango. It was almost directly below where they stood, the paintwork covered in a dull blanket of ash and soot. "Okay," he said grimly. "We go for the Durango."

There was a dozen undead wandering aimlessly along the street, shambling like lost aimless wraiths in the shadows. Cutter's eyes searched the surrounding buildings, looking for more movement.

"We can't just make a run for it," he said. "The undead will be faster. Yesterday they were shambling, but I heard a news report that said they get faster as the virus courses through to the extremities of their bodies. They'll be running today. They'll be quicker than us because we're loaded down – and there will be hundreds of them."

126

Father Bob made a face. "Maybe they've drifted out of the city," he said. "There are a few down there... but not many. Not enough that we can't handle. If we go through the front doors it's only about twenty feet to the SUV."

Cutter turned away from the window. He shook his head. "They're down there – somewhere," he insisted. "There was a swarm of them around those doors yesterday, and more at the entrance to the alley. You saw them. They haven't all just drifted away in the night. And even if some of them have, there is still going to be too many for us to deal with. We need to rely on speed and surprise. It's our only chance."

He looked up and realized Samantha was standing in the hallway, staring at him. She had changed into denim jeans and a long sleeve shirt. She had the heavy padded jacket she had worn the day before draped over her arm. She sensed the tension between her father and Cutter, and she came towards the men uncertainly. Father Bob turned and saw his daughter. He drew her towards the window.

"We're going to make a break for it this morning, honey. See the red SUV? That's what we're going to try to reach."

Samantha looked out across the street. She nodded, and then turned back to Cutter. "Do you have a plan?" she asked.

Cutter shook his head. "Not yet," he admitted. "We're going to be a slow moving target. "Between the bag of supplies, the weapons and ...." he cut himself off abruptly, but not before Father Bob sensed what he was about to say.

"I won't slow you down, Cutter," the man said. He drew himself upright, but the pain was still there, burning behind the man's steady eyes. "I know what my priorities are."

There was an unspoken moment of tension, and then Samantha turned back to the window and stared along the street again. When she faced Cutter, her expression was suddenly clouded with thought.

"What if we create a diversion?" she offered, speaking slowly as the plan formulated itself. "If you were downstairs, and you suddenly rattled and opened the front doors of the apartment – let the zombies know you were there... they'd come for you. They'd all come from wherever they are hiding. You'd be the bait," she said. Then she turned to her father. "And if daddy was out on the fire escape, and I was waiting for you at the fire escape door, you could lead them into the building. Then we run down the fire escape, and get to the SUV through the alley."

Cutter sat down on the sofa and thought hard. In his mind he visualized the response of the undead. Samantha was right. If he showed himself, they would come like a wave of death for him. He realized he would have to be quick. He would have to get up the three flights of stairs and then slip out through the fire door before any of the undead reached him. Maybe they could wedge the fire door shut from the outside just in case...

He thought then about clambering down the iron stairs and landings, and scurrying over the dumpsters blockading the entrance to the alley. If Samantha's idea worked, the undead would be surging though the apartment block. They might just make it.

If they were lucky.

He went back to the window and took one long final look at the scene of devastation and death down on the street. Somewhere in the morning sky – blocked from view by the buildings – he could hear the distant sound of a helicopter. Cutter made up his mind.

"Okay," he said. "Let's do it."

* * *

They filled up on cans of cold spaghetti and drank as much water as they could. As they ate, they re-worked Samantha's plan – adding to, and altering the basic plot as new thoughts came to them and initial ideas were discarded. While they schemed, Father Bob sat – his brow furrowed in concentration – and reloaded the Glock they had found in Walker's apartment, and the one Cutter had brought with him. There was still half a box of ammunition remaining. He stowed it in the canvas bag alongside the ammunition he had for his revolver. He handed one of the Glock's to Cutter and the other to Samantha.

When they all were in agreement – and armed – Cutter led them downstairs to the foyer.

The ground floor apartments were still being renovated. Cutter broke into 1B and 1C, ransacking the units for anything useful. There wasn't much. He found a saw, some builder's plaster – and a plastic bottle of paint thinners. He took the bottle with him and went to stare out through the main entry doors.

When the terror had begun, Father Bob and Samantha had locked the doors and barricaded part of the foyer with chairs, bookcases and tables. Cutter left the blockade in place and went up the stairs to the first floor.

He broke into the apartment closest to the stairwell and dragged a two-seat sofa through the doorway. Samantha lent a hand and together they positioned the piece of furniture at the top of the stairs.

"Just in case," Cutter explained. "If they come after me and they get too close, I'll use the thinners and set the sofa on fire. I can push it across the stairs to block the route, and buy me a little time."

Father Bob nodded. The trio went up the next flight of stairs and found a bookcase in one of the deserted units. They heaved it into position beside the stairwell and then retreated to the top floor.

Cutter went into the apartment and retrieved the bag. It was heavy. Beside food, water, and ammunition, Samantha had packed candles and a blanket. He carried it out into the passageway towards the fire-door.

"I'll take this outside and down to the first floor landing," Cutter said. He looked at Father Bob. "Your job is to be ready. When Sam and I come down those stairs, you need to be set to go." The pastor nodded. By taking the canvas bag down to the jump-off point, Cutter was saving himself a few precious seconds of time.

When he came back up the fire escape, Cutter was beginning to sweat. The morning was warm and sunny. He dragged his hand across his brow.

Samantha was waiting for him. She had a couple of dinner knifes in her hand. Cutter looked alarmed.

"I don't want them to get that close," he said in horror. "And I don't know how much harm I can do with a butter knife!"

Samantha shook her head. "I was thinking they might be a way of wedging the fire door closed after we start down the escape," she explained. "It might hold them for a few seconds – if they get that close."

Cutter thought for a moment and then nodded. He doubted they would be an effective door-jam – but he couldn't think of a better alternative. "Okay," he said. "Just make sure you keep this door open once I step out onto the sidewalk," he said.

Samantha nodded gravely. 'How will I know where you are, or how close they are to you once they chase you into the building?"

"You'll know," Cutter said, sounding like a man condemned. "Because you'll hear me screaming."

* * *

Cutter went down to the foyer and pulled two chairs away from the barricaded furniture to clear a narrow path to the door. Then he doused everything in paint thinners – emptying half the bottle's contents over sofas, cabinets, desks, tables and bookcases. The fumes hung in the air, rippling like a heat haze.

He crossed to the foot of the stairwell and left the bottle of thinners on the bottom step. Then he went back to the front doors and stared out through the tinted glass. The street seemed deserted.

There were bolts in each door at the top and bottom. He unfastened them and finally unlocked the door.

Cutter snatched the Glock from his jeans and fumbled the cigarette lighter from his pocket. He went out onto the sidewalk, into the warm morning sunlight and stood staring.

The Durango's rear windows were splattered with dry blood. He couldn't tell whether anything moved inside the vehicle, but somehow he doubted it. Then he looked back towards the bookstore. There were bodies on the ground, scattered across the road like discarded litter, and the only movement was the dark shapes of rats, scampering from one corpse to the next in evil delight. Cutter turned and glanced towards the traffic lights.

Stillness.

And silence.

No earthly sound, and no sign of movement.

He stood for a moment longer, and then took a deep breath. He raised the Glock into the air – and fired.

The sound of the shot was deafeningly loud in the oppressive silence, ripping apart the eerie stillness, and echoing between the tall buildings. Cutter counted to three.

Nothing happened.

For a split-second he considered making a dash for the Durango. It was right there! Not twenty feet away from where he stood. The temptation was almost irresistible.

But what then?

He knew the silence couldn't last. He knew it must be shattered in the next few seconds by screaming, wailing undead. How would he rescue

Father Bob and Samantha? How could he get them to the car safely?

He shook his head. It was folly – and as if to confirm his decision, suddenly three dark shambling shapes appeared on the opposite side of the street, drawn to the crashing sound of the gunshot.

There were two women and a man. They were dirty, filthy apparitions, their bodies covered in torn tatters of material, their hair wild and stiff with gore. Their faces were streaked with blood, and they came into the sunlight with their mouths agape, their eyes wide and feral. Cutter stared at the undead.

They stared back, unmoving.

Cutter pointed the pistol at one of the women. She was standing on the opposite sidewalk, swaying mindlessly from side to side. Cutter had a shot between the abandoned cars. He took careful aim and fired.

He missed. The bullet went well wide, smashing a shop front window.

Cutter swore. He adjusted his aim and took another long breath. He could feel his arm wavering, unused to the weight of the weapon. He closed one eye... and then suddenly the entire sidewalk around the undead filled with a swarm of similar dark shapes, like an army appearing from the morning mist on an ancient battlefield.

They came from the buildings. They came from the shadows into the glaring warm sunlight – and they came at a run.

The street suddenly filled with the demented wail of hundreds of undead voices, clamoring and screeching in hideous fury. Cutter turned back for the open doors of the building and ran.

More dark shapes came from his left, moving to intercept him. They spilled onto the sidewalk and burst towards him, their arms and legs flailing as they closed on their prey.

Cutter crashed back through the doors and leaped the barricade. He dropped to his knees and flicked the lighter, focusing all his attention on the task. It wouldn't light.

He heard the sound, like a storm surging closer. He glanced up and the glass façade of the building was suddenly enveloped in shadow as the undead filled the sidewalk.

"Concentrate!"

He flicked the lighter again – and a table and sofa erupted into flames with a sudden *'whoosh!'*

Cutter didn't pause. He scrambled to his feet and threw himself at the stairs. Behind him he could hear the crackling sound of the fire as it leaped across the entrance. He could feel the intense heat on his back. And he could hear the sudden sounds of glass smashing and the shrieks of the zombies as they spilled into the foyer and were confronted with a solid wall of flame.

He snatched up the bottle of thinners and took the stairs two-at-a-time. The noise behind him rose to a crescendo. He reached the top of the stairwell and glanced over his shoulder.

The zombies were surging into the foyer, moving like a dark wave. The press of their momentum was impossible to stop, forcing the first ones through the doorway onto the wall of flames. Their clothes and hair caught alight and they spun and flailed their wretched burning bodies in wild confusion. Some fell into the barricade and became part of the erupting blaze. Other crashed through and staggered like fiery torches into the ransacked ground floor apartments. The whole foyer became filled with flame – and still the press of the demented filled the sidewalk beyond.

Then they saw Cutter through the fire and billowing smoke – and a hundred undead voices suddenly shrieked with malevolent fury. They hurled themselves at the flames, driven by insane madness, and the barricade blew apart in an explosion of shattering timbers and burning embers.

Cutter leaped the final steps onto the landing and splashed lighter fluid over the sofa that he and Samantha had prepared. The fabric burst into sudden flames and he heaved at it with his foot until it reached the point of balance, and began to slide down the stairwell.

He turned and ran.

The whole apartment block was going up in flames, and the heat rising up from the foyer was intense. Paint began to blister on the walls and he heard pounding footsteps behind him, sounding like the maddened beat of a thousand drums. He pushed himself on, driven by fear and panic. The footsteps came closer, became louder, and when he reached the second story landing he turned to see one of the undead staring up at him from the bottom of the stairs. The thing was hideously deformed. Once it had been a man, but now it was a disfigured wraith. It was naked, its body blackened and festering with running sores and open wounds. Its head was grotesquely swollen, and the fire had burned away its hair and eyelids and lips so that all that remained was smoldering melted skin. It hissed at Cutter, and then suddenly vomited thick black bile. Cutter stared in horror. The sickly sweet stench of burning flesh swept over him, mingled with the fetid odor of rotting corruption. Cutter drew the Glock and fired.

The bullet hit the zombie between the eyes and it was flung backwards down the stairs. It fell into the path of other undead and was crushed beneath their pounding feet.

Cutter pulled the bookcase across the stairwell as a final barricade. He threw the bottle of thinners over it and set it alight. The sudden wall of heat hit him like a shock wave. He reeled back, the air sucked from his lungs, and the side of his face suddenly stinging hot. For a split-second he thought he had been burned. His vision suddenly clouded, and then he realized it was thick smoke choking up from the ground floor. He went up the final set of stairs holding his breath, and his eyes streaming with tears.

Samantha was standing at the open fire-door. He saw her as he reached the landing. He ran towards her.

She was screaming at him. He could see the horror in her face but the roar of the burning building and the demented wail of the pursuing zombies drowned her words out. Cutter felt himself stumbling. He felt his legs becoming leaden. He sensed the wave of ghouls closing in behind him so that the reek of death seemed to hang over his shoulder like an executioner's axe.

His feet went from under him. He dropped to his knees and rolled. His hands clawed at the carpet. Then he was suddenly on his feet again, stumbling through the choking smoke, and Samantha was at his side, dragging him by his arm and leading him towards the blue sky and fresh air that waited beyond the fire door.

Cutter went reeling through the door and hung over the iron railing. His lungs burned. He was coughing and choking. He felt himself swaying with dizzy disorientation. Behind him he heard Samantha grunting. The fire door slammed closed, and she kicked at the handles of the knives to wedge the door shut. Then she snatched at Cutter's arm and flung him towards the stairs.

"Come on!" she screamed. "They were right behind you!"

Cutter stumbled down the narrow fire escape, clinging to the railing, his body still racked with heaving spasms of coughing. His clothes hung from him, drenched with sweat, and there was a pounding pain in his head. He pushed himself on, hearing Samantha's frantic urging loud in his ears.

Father Bob was waiting at the bottom landing, and the canvas carry bag was at the man's feet. He extended the ladder to the ground and pushed Samantha ahead of himself.

"You go!" Father Bob said.

Samantha didn't hesitate. She scrambled towards the ground and leaped the last few yards, landing on her feet.

"Now you!" Father Bob pushed Cutter in the back. "I'll drop the bag down to you."

Cutter swarmed down the ladder. Behind him he heard a sudden loud crash. He looked up in alarm. There were zombies standing at the top of the fire escape. They saw Samantha and Cutter on the ground and they shrieked in murderous rage.

"Come on!" Cutter shouted to Father Bob.

The big man heaved the bag over the railing and Cutter caught it in two hands, the weight of it staggering him backwards. Then he heard the loud crash of a gunshot. Father Bob had drawn the revolver from his coat. He fired three shots at the zombies. One of them sagged against the railing and didn't move again.

"Move it!" Cutter screamed. The pastor fired one more shot and then came down the fire escape, his panic making him awkward. When he hit the ground he heaved the ladder back up, and then they turned and ran desperately into the alleyway.

* * *

They got ten paces. That was all.

Then suddenly behind them, Cutter heard a sickening crack of breaking bones and a snarling howl of fury. He spun around. One of the zombies had hurled itself over the fire escape railing. The ghoul had landed face-first on the concrete. Its body was twisted at an impossible angle, but its head rose up from the ground and its hands clawed at him. The zombie's face had been crushed beyond recognition, but still the malevolent fury blazed in its eyes. Cutter dropped the bag and doubled back. He put a single round into the zombie's head from point-blank range and then flung himself sideways as a second body plummeted to the ground. It landed just a few feet away; the body of a woman. It landed feet-first, and the crushing impact splintered and fractured every bone in its legs. Thick brown slime spilled across the pavement. Cutter shot the woman between the eyes and dashed back towards the alley.

They reached the dumpsters that blocked the alley entrance, and Cutter hurled himself at the obstacle, scrambling up onto bags of rubbish until he could see the street beyond. His heart was pounding in his chest and his hands were clammy with fear.

They had a clear path to the Durango. He helped Samantha over the dumpster and then Father Bob heaved the bag up to him. Cutter passed it down to where Samantha stood and then helped the pastor over the obstacle.

They dropped to the ground together, crouched against the side wall of the apartment building.

"You go straight for the car," Cutter said to Samantha. "Your father and I will cover you. Once you get there, check the back seat, for God's sake. Thump on the window. They're drawn to noise. If anything is still inside you will know it. If the car is clear, get in behind the wheel and get it started. Understand?"

Samantha nodded. She glanced at her father for a brief second and she smiled bravely. Father Bob put his hand on her shoulder and squeezed. He grinned to reassure her. "I'll be right behind you, honey. Promise."

Samantha went across the street doubled over and running as fast as she could. She was light on her feet. Cutter swung the Glock to cover the entrance of the apartment block and Father Bob knelt beside him, sweeping the revolver in an arc to cover the opposite side of the road.

Samantha got to the Durango and pounded her fist on the windows of the vehicle. She glanced over her shoulder at Cutter – and then flung the driver's door wide open.

Cutter waited. His nerves were drawn tight. His eyes flicked away from the entrance of the building to the Durango. He heard the engine whine and then burble to life. Cutter let out a long breath of relief. He thumped Father Bob's shoulder.

"Go!" Cutter said. "Take the bag, and get in the back seat. I've got you covered."

The pastor nodded. He went at a loping shuffle, weighed down by the canvas bag, and as he ran his head swiveled from side to side looking for threats. Cutter followed him with his eyes until the pastor finally reached the car.

There was blood across the back seats. Father Bob scrambled into the vehicle. A moment later Cutter saw the rear window slide down and the older man's face appeared, red and gasping. He gave Cutter a 'thumbs-up' sign.

Cutter could hear the Durango's engine idling steadily over the noise of the burning building. There were still dark shapes milling around the entrance, but the frenzy in them had dulled. They began to wander away from the apartment block in aimless shuffles. Cutter knew that every second he hesitated increased the danger of being discovered. He pushed himself to his feet and sprinted for the Durango.

It was twenty feet to the car, and another few seconds to get around the hood and into the passenger seat. He went in a hunched jinking run, his eyes fixed on Samantha's face framed behind the windshield.

He heard the engine revving as he got closer. His eyes swept the shaded sidewalk on the opposite side of the street. Over his shoulder he heard a sudden loud explosive crash as though the apartment block was collapsing.

He didn't look back. He didn't dare. He noticed Father Bob's face in the back seat. The man's eyes were suddenly wide and fearful. Cutter saw him thrust the revolver out through the window aiming past his shoulder. The man was shouting at him but Cutter couldn't hear. The only sounds were the slap of his boots on the tarmac and the sawing of his breath, deafeningly loud in his ears.

He reached the hood of the Durango. Felt the warmth of the engine under the bonnet. Spun himself around the grille and his fingers groped desperately for the door handle.

Then Father Bob fired.

The blast of the shot was hugely loud – a sound that ripped through the silence on the street. Cutter glanced up. He saw one of the undead running towards the Durango. He flung the car door open and threw himself inside.

"Go!" he shouted at Samantha. The ghoul was just a few yards away. He heard the pastor fire again and the roar was deafening. The zombie went down in a spinning heap. It collapsed against the trunk of a nearby car and fell slowly to the ground.

"Go now!" Cutter screamed.

Samantha tightened her grip on the steering wheel and slammed her foot on the gas pedal. The car leaped forward and she had to wrench the wheel down hard to swing the SUV up onto the sidewalk. Other undead had been drawn from the burning building by the gunfire. A dozen – maybe more – suddenly came snarling at a run from within the fiery building. They had once been men and women and children. Now they were the undead – possessed of nothing but mindless seething rage. Samantha mowed them down, her jaw set in a determined line, her teeth gritted as body after body crashed against the hood and fenders and went reeling away. One of the ghouls leaped onto the car and smashed its head into the windshield. Samantha screamed. The zombie raised its head like a cobra and lunged again. The windshield starred into a sheet of tiny opaque diamonds.

Samantha spun the wheel hard. There was a bench seat on the sidewalk. The Durango went crashing into it, staving in the driver's side fender with such a shuddering impact that the undead shape was thrown from the vehicle. Samantha slammed the Durango into reverse and the tires burned blue smoke and rubber. She spun the wheel again, and crashed back onto the street. The corner rushed towards them, just a few seconds more. There was another jarring shudder that seemed to shake the whole car.

"Cover your eyes," Cutter shouted, and then punched his fist through the windshield. Chips of glass flew back into Samantha's face and hair. Cutter punched again until the hole he had made with his fist was enough for Samantha to see through.

"Now floor it!"

The intersection was right on top of them and Samantha dragged the wheel over, skidding into the turn, and clipping one of the traffic light poles as the off-side wheels went up onto the sidewalk then crashed down onto solid road again.

They were on a short narrow side street, and Cutter could see the next turn in the road racing towards them. He wrenched himself around in his seat and stared over his shoulder. A swarm of ghouls were racing after the vehicle, running and snarling.

"If you slow down for this corner they'll catch us and we're all dead," he told Samantha.

* * *

The Durango took the sharp turn at full speed, swinging wide onto the opposite side of the road as the tires squealed in a protest of burning rubber. The vehicle handled like a boat; rolling and swaying as Samantha corrected quickly. A garbage truck filled the windscreen. It had been abandoned. The driver's side door was open. Samantha stabbed her foot at the brake to bleed off speed and flung the wheel hard over. The Durango clipped the truck's open door and then veered onto the right side of the road.

"Slow down," Cutter said with the sort of calmness in his voice that was entirely forced. "We're away from them. They've stopped chasing." He reached across and touched one of Samantha's white-knuckled hands. "Ease off the gas," he continued to encourage her. "The last thing we want now is to have a collision."

The road was four lanes wide – the major artery that led out of the city. Shops lined both sides of the street, but it was the old part of town, and many of them had been abandoned in recent years and attacked by graffiti vandals. Cars were parked up along the curb, and more were strewn across the lanes of traffic – abandoned by their drivers when the terror had struck and people had fled for their lives.

Samantha slowed until the car was cruising. The street was like an obstacle course, and she veered across all four lanes as trucks, buses and family sedans made their progress into a careful slalom. They were surrounded by death and destruction. A bus was slewed across two lanes. It had crashed into a traffic light. The steel pole had snapped at the point of impact and lay across the road. The bus's windows were streaked with blood and the emergency exit window at the rear of the vehicle lay shattered on the nearby sidewalk. There were hundreds of cars, all of them deserted. Many of them damaged, or sprayed with gore. Samantha drove cautiously, with her eyes fixed on the road ahead, as though she couldn't bear to comprehend the devastation that surrounded her.

They were silent and somber as they drove towards the edge of the city.

The arterial road branched off in a major intersection, with turns to the north and south, but as they drew closer they realized the corner was littered with more deserted cars. Some of them had been burned out. Several of the vehicles had collided and one had caught ablaze and still smoldered.

There were bodies too.

Not many – but enough.

They lay on the street and on the sidewalk in desperate attitudes of panic and despair. Some lay dead with their bodies flung against walls, or hanging limp and lifeless from the open doors of their vehicles. Others had been crushed. Cutter saw the shapes of two young children, and beside them was the silhouette of a crashed Mazda. The vehicle had mounted the sidewalk and buried itself into the front of a pizza shop – leaving the mangled tiny bodies of the children snagged under its rear tires.

The morning was still – the silence like a heavy weight that bore down on them – as they drove past one horror and then discovered another, until the tragedy and the despair crushed their spirit and left them grim-faced and desolate.

In the back seat, Cutter heard father Bob muttering prayers for the dead, whilst beside him Samantha wept silent tears. Cutter clenched his jaw and stared ahead through the shattered windshield, clamping down on his despair – because it was the only way he could deal with the horror and still go on.

They reached the intersection and Samantha slowed the SUV to a crawl. "We want to go north," Cutter said. The intersection was jammed solid. Samantha stopped the car.

"How?" she asked. She leaned forward and stared through the shattered glass. There was a bus stopped at an angle across the intersection and behind it a cab that had flipped and rolled onto its side wedged against the crushed shape of an old pick up. Behind the carnage were more vehicles in every lane and others that had been abandoned on the median strip as drivers had sought to find a desperate way through the traffic before forsaking their cars altogether.

"The sidewalk," Cutter pointed.

There was an electrical store on the corner. It was a two-story brick building. The glass shop front windows had been smashed and Cutter could see a slumped body. The store had been looted. Out front

145

was a traffic sign, showing distances to the surrounding suburbs. Cutter nodded. "Run it down."

Samantha glanced at him and trapped her lip between her teeth.

"Are you serious?"

Cutter nodded. "It's the only way."

"You want me to mount the sidewalk and crash through the sign?"

"Yes." Cutter said. "Because if we can't get through this intersection we can't reach Eden Gardens."

Still Samantha hesitated. "There might be another way... Another turnoff that would be easier."

"There is no easy way," Cutter insisted. "This is the *only* way."

Samantha backed the SUV up and revved the engine. The noise in the silence was unusually loud. Rats scurried away from the bodies they were devouring and dark shaped crows took to sudden raucous flight.

Samantha slipped the car into gear and crushed the gas pedal under her foot.

The Durango leaped forward, gathering speed quickly. It mounted the curb with a sudden jarring thump that flung them forward in their seats. Samantha's arms on the wheel were locked. The car bucked wildly, bouncing high and hard on its springs, then settled back onto all four wheels. A split second later the traffic sign filled her vision and she turned her head away instinctively and closed her eyes.

"Brace yourself!" Cutter shouted.

The Durango slammed into the sign and the metal post buckled before the vehicle's momentum.

The car went up and over, and the rending crashing sound was a hugely loud explosion in their ears. The vehicle jolted and tilted, then righted itself. A second later the car crashed back down off the sidewalk and swerved onto the road – heading north – with the choked intersection suddenly behind them.

Samantha let out a breath she had been holding. Cutter heard Father Bob sigh his relief. Cutter turned round in his seat and stared through the rear window of the SUV. Dark wandering shapes were emerging onto the road, spilling from the buildings around the intersection but disappearing into the distance quickly. Cutter allowed himself the luxury of a moment's relief. The undead were slow-moving, and the car was hurtling north – approaching leafy tree-lined inner-city suburbs.

They were safely through the intersection.

They were safely out of the city.

They were on their way to Eden Gardens.

And then the car broke down.

* * *

There was no warning. The car just stopped in the middle of a wreckage-strewn road.

Samantha stared down at the dashboard in horror.

Cutter swore. "Are we out of fuel?"

Samantha shook her head. "We've still got a quarter tank," she turned to him and her eyes were huge and dark, filled with fear. She thumped the steering wheel, then tried to start the car again. The

147

engine whirred and died. She stomped her foot on the gas pedal and tried again.

The car sat dead on the road.

Cutter snatched a glance through the rear window. The distant shapes of shuffling undead were moving towards them, suddenly seeming to be filled with malicious awareness. He saw more dark shapes come from buildings, and he swore again.

"Get out!" he snapped. "We've got to find another car – and we've got to do it in a hurry."

They tumbled from the Durango. Cutter was seething. There was no time. The dark wall of shuffling undead was drawing closer, their figures seeming to ripple in the morning heat haze that rose off the blacktop. He looked around in frantic desperation.

There were other abandoned cars scattered on the road. He slapped Samantha on the back.

"We can outrun them – but not for ever. Not with this bag. They'll hunt us down eventually. So go and find something that has fuel," he urged her, and she turned and ran further along the street towards a couple of compact Japanese sedans.

Father Bob dragged the heavy canvas bag from the Durango and dropped it onto the road. He went down on one knee beside the trunk of the SUV and glanced over his shoulder at Cutter.

"I'll hold them off," the pastor said. The older man looked ill, and between words his face contorted into a grimace of sudden silent pain.

Cutter nodded. He handed his Glock to the big man and then turned and stared.

There were houses on either side of the street. They were big brick residences, owned by wealthy locals who could afford to live close to the heart of the city. They had beautifully manicured lawns and ornate decorative windows. Some of them had cars parked in driveways. Cutter ran towards the closest house.

It was an older-style home: a red-brick two-story building with a gabled roof and lead-light windows on the ground floor. The curtains were drawn tight, and he noticed that two of the west-facing windows had aluminum security shutters to block out the afternoon heat.

Cutter paused for a split second, and considered making a stand. The home looked secure...

He glanced back along the road towards the intersection. The zombies were shambling closer. The group was splintering apart as the faster moving ghouls broke away from the rest of the group. They were a hundred yards away from the Durango.

Cutter ran down the driveway. There was a brick garage at the end of a cobblestoned path, and parked in front was a Volvo wagon. Cutter tried the driver-side door. It was locked. He spun around in wild desperation, looking for a weapon to smash the window.

He ran into the garage.

There was a narrow work-bench along the back wall of the structure, and above it was a wide stretch of peg-board filled with tools: hammers, saws and screwdrivers. There were more shelves to his left, and an old wardrobe that had once been a beautiful bedroom piece. Now it was a storage area for paints, brushes and gardening tools. Cutter found a small axe and picked it up.

He ran back towards the Volvo. He could hear the wail of the zombies out on the street. A dense green hedge of manicured bushes blocked his view of the Durango, but the shrill sound of the undead was rising.

He carried the axe back to the Volvo and hefted it over his shoulder to strike.

That was how he saw the open door.

There was a rear-entrance to the home – a green timber door at the top of three concrete steps. The door was open. Cutter paused. He lowered the axe and went towards the door cautiously.

He crept up the steps and pushed the door open wide with the head of the axe. Stood in the darkened gloom for long seconds while his eyes adjusted to the light.

He was standing in a kitchen. There was a table to his left, set with dinner plates and half-eaten meals. Flies filled the air, buzzing in angry swarms like a thick cloud. Seated around the table were a man, a woman and a child. The woman and the child were slumped back in their seats, their eyes wide and staring. The woman had a bullet hole in the center of her forehead. The child was a girl. She was dressed in a school uniform. She had long black hair and an expression of shock on her face. A bullet had smashed through one of her eyes sockets and the back of her head had collapsed.

Cutter gaped in horror.

Then the man at the table turned towards him.

He was middle-aged. He had black hair, quickly turning grey. He had a thin, drawn face, and his eyes were small and very dark. He looked like an accountant, or maybe a lawyer. He stared at Cutter and his mouth fell open, slack.

"Are you the gardener?" the man asked numbly. His voice croaked. Cutter took a step back. The stench of death in the room hit him. He shook his head.

The man scraped back his chair and got slowly to his feet. There was a pistol on the table next to a dinner plate that swarmed with flies and wriggling maggots. The man's trousers were covered in urine and feces.

He picked up a napkin, moving in a slow dazed trance, and dabbed at the corner of his lips. He smiled at Cutter, and his expression was almost weary. Then he leaned over and kissed the dead woman's open mouth. A fly crawled across the woman's cold lips and disappeared into the cavity of her nose. The man didn't seem to notice. "I'll be home about six," he said softly. He turned to his daughter. "Be a good girl at school, okay?"

He waited for the dead girl to answer, and when she didn't the man frowned. He turned to Cutter again and shrugged.

"Kids. She's a teenager," the man said as if that explained everything. "She's got an attitude that's a mile wide."

Cutter backed away towards the door. He raised the axe and held it ready across his chest. The man suddenly seemed to recognize the pistol. He picked it up and placed it carefully under his chin.

Cutter stumbled out through the door. Nausea scalded the back of his throat and he tripped down the stairs and fell against the wall of the house. He shook his head like a man in a daze.

He heard the loud roar of the gunshot, and then a second later he heard the man's body fall to the floor.

Then he heard more gunshots – these ones coming from the road in a sporadic hail of fire. Cutter turned and ran for the Durango.

There were four undead ghouls lying on the road, not fifteen feet away from the Durango. Cutter hurdled a low brick wall and ran into the middle of the street. The zombie wave was undulating and writhing – maybe fifty ghouls shambling and reaching out for the pastor. Cutter dropped to his haunches behind the big man and took back the Glock. He snapped off two shots.

"Where's Samantha?"

The pastor shook his head. The closest undead were maybe a dozen feet away from the Durango. Cutter turned and looked for the girl, and then looked for an escape.

"We've got to move," he urged the pastor.

Father Bob shook his head. "We won't get clear of them with the bag," he said. "It's too late for that." He fired off a shot at the face of a woman zombie who was snarling at him. The woman's wretched eyes were yellow and wide with her frenzy. She took one more convulsive shambling step and collapsed to the ground unmoving.

"Well we can't stay here!" Cutter shouted.

Father Bob turned to Cutter and there was a sudden peace and tranquility in his expression. The big man smiled, and Cutter saw that same sparkle of compassion and faith in the man's eyes he had recognized the instant they had met.

"I can, Jack," Father Bob said calmly. "It's you who needs to escape. Take the bag. Go and find my baby girl. Get her to safety for me."

Cutter stared with sudden incredulous disbelief. "No," Cutter said. "We go now, and we go together."

152

Father Bob reached out and squeezed Cutter's shoulder. "Please," he said. "Do this for me. I'm a dead man anyhow, Jack. We both know that. It's just a matter of time. This way, I get to choose my time. This way I get to do what's right – not die wasting away as a burden to anyone. It's right – you know it is."

Cutter shook his head. One of the undead staggered against the Durango, so close that Cutter could smell the reeking stench of the decaying corpse. He flung the Glock up and fired a desperate shot that snapped the undead ghoul's head back. The zombie collapsed to the ground and the others trampled over it.

"Go now!" Father Bob pleaded. "Before it's too late for both of us."

Cutter shook his head defiantly. "I can't do that," he said. He snatched hold of the canvas bag and got to his feet. He reached for the pastor and dragged him back until they were standing at the hood of the Durango.

The wall of undead pressed closer, like a remorseless, relentless tide of death that could not be stopped: could not be turned back. Father Bob smiled serenely and then placed the revolver in Cutter's hand.

"Tell Sam I love her," he said. Then he turned away and hurled himself into the clamoring wall of wretched dead. Cutter cried out – but it was too late. The zombies attacked and mutilated the pastor in an instant of frenzied maddened rage as the ghouls gouged and shredded his body. Cutter heard the pastor scream – but it was not a cry of pain or terror.

Somehow – to Cutter's ears – it was the sound of freedom.

Cutter staggered backwards. Turned his head away. There were tears welling up in his eyes and he blinked them away. He picked up the bag and began to run, but his legs were leaden. He heard the sound of a revving engine and turned blindly. Samantha was behind the wheel of a silver Honda hatchback. She hammered her fist on the horn and leaned out through the open window.

"Come on!" she screamed. Cutter ran. He hurled the heavy bag into the car and dived into the passenger seat.

"Where is my father?" Samantha asked with a dull sense of premonition. Her voice was suddenly hollow – empty of all emotion.

Cutter stared ahead, and for an instant the sound of the terrible wailing and the imminent sense of danger and panic seemed to dissolve away.

"He's not coming with us," Cutter said.

Samantha turned to Cutter, and then looked back over her shoulder at the undead ghouls that filled the street. Many were covered with fresh blood. It dripped from their chins and left fresh stains on their ragged clothes.

Samantha nodded. She eased her foot down on the gas pedal and the little car nosed past a wrecked station wagon. Ahead of them the road opened into four lanes of empty highway.

Samantha drove away in stoic sobbing anguish – heading for the Garden of Eden.

Five.
The highway.

Samantha drove with exaggerated caution. The car crawled along the blacktop, gradually leaving the smoldering ruined city behind until it was just a dark burning shape in the rear view mirror.

The highway ahead stretched like an undulating ribbon into the distance, littered with the debris of mangled and abandoned vehicles. Everywhere they looked was death and destruction.

They cruised past a school bus that had been abandoned, with its front wheels slewed across two lanes. The rear of the bus had crashed into a steel guardrail. The windows on one side of the bus had been shattered so that glass was sprayed across the road. Cutter saw limp, lifeless young bodies still in their seats and blood dripped down the side of the bus to puddle on the gravel. The driver had been thrown head-first through the windshield and lay on the hood of the bus, his body twisted at an impossible angle, his eyes wide open and staring as though in utter disbelief. A huge black crow was perched on the man's back. The bird stared at Cutter as the car crept past, and then went back to chewing at the dead bus driver's body.

Every hundred yards was a new, chilling horror.

They saw an overturned car with the dead driver still pinned under the wreckage of the vehicle. It was a young woman. Her legs had been crushed, and she lay on the roadside in a puddle of her own blood. Her hands and fingers were a shocking gored mangle, as though she had died trying to claw herself to safety. Two crows were feeding on her body. One was perched on the back of the woman's head, nibbling at the soft flesh of her neck. The other was settled on her back, tearing through the blood-soaked remnants of the woman's blouse. And they saw an old man, sitting on the side of the highway, his back resting against a metal post. The man was staring up at the afternoon sun, his head thrown back in an attitude of bewilderment. Rats had come from the grassy verge and were gnawing at the old man's legs, lacerating the paper-thin skin and feasting on his feet and toes. Cutter didn't know if the man was still alive – and they didn't stop the car to find out.

Slowly the miles dragged on, and as the afternoon began to darken, the constant horrors beat down upon their senses until they became numb and immune to the carnage so that they slowed less often – gaped and shuddered less frequently.

"We're not going to make Eden Gardens before nightfall," Cutter said at last. Samantha looked at him, her expression sharp with alarm. Cutter glanced through the windshield at the setting sun. Dark storm clouds were boiling on the horizon.

He had no idea what time it was – maybe four or five o'clock. Long shadows stretched across the highway.

"And I don't want to be on this road at night," he said.

He hadn't been this far north of Newbridge for years, but he had a vague recollection of a roadside gas station at the turnoff to Draketown. He told Samantha.

"It can't be much further," Cutter said.

The highway north of the city had been upgraded and re-aligned in the last decade and he leaned forward in his seat, trying to see past the debris, anticipating the sight of the little general store as each new bend in the road slowly appeared. Twenty minutes later he saw it.

It was very different to the way he remembered. The old weatherboard building with a couple of weary gas pumps on a half-acre of roadside gravel was gone, and in its place had been built something altogether different.

The land had been concreted, and marked with painted lines for parking bays. Cutter saw a dozen cars sitting empty in the afternoon light.

The old building had been torn down and replaced with a diner, set well back from the road. There were long full-length glass windows across the front shaded under an aluminum awning. The walls were brick and covered with Coca Cola signs. Closer to the highway was a bank of four gas pumps. There was a car parked up alongside one of the pumps. The driver's door was open, and the vehicle was empty.

Cutter began to feel uneasy. The building he remembered might have been a safe, defendable haven to rest for the night. A glass-fronted diner was not. He felt his hopes begin to slide as the silver hatchback slowly crept closer.

Cutter looked around carefully, his eyes searching for signs of movement – for any sense of danger.

He noticed about a dozen houses that had been built just beyond the turnoff to Draketown.

They were new. They all looked the same: like some small random estate of cookie-cutter homes that had been thrown up quickly by a developer who had been keen to make a fast buck with low cost accommodation. Cutter frowned, and his sense of disquiet started to sound louder in the back of his mind.

The old gas station had stood alone in the middle of nowhere – just a dot on the map beside a turn in the road. Now he was staring at a small residential development. Cutter wondered about the homes, and what might be waiting for them as the night pressed down and the darkness filled with sounds and fear.

"Is this the place?" Samantha asked. She sounded scared.

"I'm not sure anymore," Cutter admitted. "It's changed a lot from the way I remembered it."

Samantha stopped the car in the middle of the highway, forty yards short of the diner. She left the motor running and glanced down at the temperature and fuel gauge needles. She bit her lip. "Car's getting a little hot," she said softly. They had been driving at such low speed the radiator had begun to hiss under the hood. "And we have a little under half a tank of gas left."

Cutter nodded. Half a tank of gas was all they needed – Eden Gardens couldn't be more than twenty miles ahead. But the radiator was a problem.

He turned to Samantha. "What do you think?"

The girl stared through the windscreen, anxiety darkening her expression. "I don't like it," she said at last.

Cutter nodded. "Neither do I. But I don't see what choice we have. We can't drive through the night."

Samantha nodded. "But maybe there will be somewhere else we can stop," she offered. "There might be another place further along the road. Maybe a farmhouse, or another general store."

"And if there isn't?"

Samantha sat back in the driver's seat. Cutter could see the rise and fall of her chest and the movement of her breasts beneath the fabric of her shirt as she fought to control her breathing. Finally she turned to him with sad, fatalistic eyes. She nodded. "Okay," she said in a small voice, and Cutter sensed the girl had suddenly remembered that she was alone with him – that her father was no longer there to protect her.

For the first time in her life she was alone in the world.

Cutter had re-loaded the revolver and the Glock during the drive. He put the revolver in the glove compartment and racked back the slide on the Glock.

"Just go in nice and easy," Cutter said. "Whatever you do, don't stop the car. Don't park up anywhere. We want to cruise around the parking bay for a few minutes. If there's anything waiting for us, we'll have time to get away."

Samantha nodded grimly. She tightened her grip on the wheel. Cutter slid down the passenger-side window and felt a cool breeze on his face. He braced himself in the seat, tensing his body and feeling his nerves suddenly string taut. The car rolled off the blacktop and he heard the tires crunch over loose gravel as it bumped down onto the concrete.

They drove past the front of the diner warily. Samantha's eyes darted anxiously in all directions. Cutter stared through the glass windows.

The diner was gloomy – and deserted.

He could see about a dozen tables, and twice as many chairs, strewn around the room, upended or laying on their side. Against the far wall he could make out the shape of a high serving counter. A cash register was lying open. The floor was littered with napkins and cutlery. There was blood on the bottom of the diner's door. Nothing moved.

Samantha reached the far end of the parking lot and pulled the car into a tight three-point turn. They cruised back the way they had come.

"Stop." Cutter said when the car was near the glass door. "Wait here – and keep the motor running."

Before Samantha could protest, he flung himself out of the Honda and crouched, poised. He reached slowly for the door and pulled it wide open. The stench washed over him like a wave: the familiar sickly reek of death, mingled with the greasy smell of fried food and coffee. Cutter used a chair to keep the door wedged open and stepped past spattered blood that lay slick and congealing on the tiled floor.

He stood inside the diner for long seconds. The place felt abandoned. He saw a stand of packaged snack food to his left and he snatched up bags of potato chips. The sound was loud in the eerie silence and he swung the gun in an arc towards an open door behind the serving counter.

There was a wide hole in the wall next to the doorway and beyond he could see the shiny steel edges of commercial cooking equipment.

Cutter stomped his foot loudly on the floor. Nothing moved. No sound. He scraped a chair across the tiles. The sound was jarringly loud. He let it fall to the ground and the noise echoed around the empty walls.

He waited. Nothing.

Finally he allowed himself a long slow breath. He turned to Samantha, sitting fraught with panic in the waiting car. He raised his thumb and edged backwards out through the door until he felt the fender of the Honda brush against his leg. Without taking his eyes off the empty diner he called quietly over his shoulder.

"It's empty," he said. "Park the car up between a couple of the others. Reverse it into a space so the nose is out. We're going to spend the night here."

He heard Samantha sigh, and then the sound of the car revving. Samantha swung the Honda into a parking space and Cutter edged back into the middle of the concrete lot to meet her as she came running to him. "What about the bag?" she asked. Cutter nodded. He handed his Glock to Samantha and fetched the bag from the car. He hefted it over his shoulder, took his gun back and waited until Samantha had drawn the other Glock from her jeans. "And the revolver?"

"I left it," Cutter said. "And I left the car unlocked. Just in case we need to get away quickly."

Samantha shook her head. "What?" she sounded appalled. "It might get stolen. Then what will we do?"

"There are plenty of other cars here," he said. "If anyone comes in the night and they're looking for a car to steal, a little Honda hatchback won't be their first choice. And it's worth the risk for us to be able to escape quickly."

Side-by-side, with the pistols drawn, they edged back towards the diner. Around them night was falling fast. The warmth of the sun had gone, leaving the air chill. Samantha shivered.

Cutter went though the door, moved the chair aside and held it open with his back until Samantha went into the diner ahead of him. He let the door close and locked it.

"What's beyond that door?"

"Kitchen," Cutter said. "I don't know what else."

They went cautiously around the counter. Cutter stole a glance through the doorway and ducked back. His grip on the gun tightened. He took a deep breath and stepped into the opening.

There was a man's arm on the floor. It had been hacked off from the rest of the body and lay mangled in a pool of blood. The limb was stiff and pale, and there was a bloody knife still gripped within the fingers. There was a gold watch around the wrist. Cutter followed the frenzied patterns of blood with his eyes and found the other arm lying on a stainless steel bench. The torso of the body was slumped behind a deep-frying vat on the far side of the kitchen. It was awash with blood – more blood than Cutter imagined a body could contain. He gagged and turned away. Then saw the body's head in a sink. It looked to Cutter as though the head had been severed, and then ripped from the torso. The mouth hung agape, the jaw slack. The skin was pale, the eyes wide and staring. It was the head of a middle-aged man. Cutter glanced over his shoulder at Samantha. She was edging through the kitchen door, her eyes enormous. "Don't come in here," Cutter warned. "Watch the entrance while I check out what's behind this last door."

It was a steel door without a lock, hanging ajar between two commercial refrigerators. Cutter smelt spoiling food as he stepped closer. The door was narrow. Cutter set the heavy bag at his feet and held the pistol ready. He flung it open.

It was dark inside. There was no light. He fumbled for the lighter in his jeans and flicked it on.

It was some kind of a storage room. He could smell onions and dirt. He held the lighter high overhead and stepped into the room. It was only small – maybe fifteen feet square. There were shelves stocked with boxes of rotting fruit and vegetables along one wall. Cutter went quickly back out into the blood-spattered kitchen.

"In here," he urged Samantha.

He led her into the storage room and dragged the bag in behind them. He lit a candle and pulled the door closed.

Samantha took the candle and held it high over her head. She glanced quickly at the surroundings and then back to Cutter. She shook her head. "There's no lock?"

"No."

She stared at him in appalled silence for long moments. "And you want to spend the night here?"

Cutter nodded.

"In a room without a lock on the door?"

Cutter nodded again. "It's not perfect," he conceded. "But we either sleep in here, or in the car."

"But there's no lock!" Samantha said again, her voice edged with rising hysteria.

"I know," Cutter grabbed her shoulders. "So we have to be quiet. Stealth and secrecy are going to keep us safe."

* * *

Cutter filled a plastic shopping bag with snack food and warm soft drinks and came quietly back to the storage room. Samantha was sitting cross-legged on the dirty floor, hunched and miserable. She barely looked up as Cutter began sorting through the supplies.

"It's dark out now," he said. "I checked the lock on the door and set a couple of chairs against it."

Samantha raised her eyes. "Do you think the chairs are going to stop the undead from breaking in?"

"No," Cutter said. "But the noise will at least give us some warning."

Samantha grunted. Cutter reached for the candle and set it down between them. He held up a bag of chips. "Chicken flavor, or barbeque?"

Samantha said nothing. Cutter handed her one of the packets and a can of Coke. The can was warm.

"Eat while you can," Cutter said. "You never know when we'll get the chance again."

She looked up at him. "And what about sleep?"

Cutter nodded. "You can sleep tonight," he said. "I'll stand guard at the door."

"You don't trust me to pull my share of guard duty?"

Cutter shook his head. "It's not that," he said. "You need to sleep because you're driving. I can sleep tomorrow in the car until we reach Eden Gardens."

Samantha lapsed into moody silence. Now the terror of escaping the city was just a lingering nightmare, she felt the full crushing weight of sad despondency as her memories drifted back to her father.

Cutter sat in the corner and let her be. There was nothing he could say – and he had his own dead family to grieve.

* * *

Cutter heard a harsh sound, and his nerves ripped and jangled in alarm. It was the sound of the diner's glass door being forced. He sat up, pressed his ear against the door of the storage room, and listened for long seconds with the sound of his breathing and the sudden thump of his heart drowning out the detail.

He went to where Samantha lay and shook her awake urgently. Her eyes flew alert in an instant.

Cutter put his finger to his lips. "Someone is breaking in to the diner," he whispered.

Samantha reached for her Glock and Cutter went back to the door.

The sounds were louder now, harsh scraping noises. Cutter imagined the door being wedged open and the chairs he had used as a barricade being forced aside. He felt the press of Samantha's warm thigh against his own and he turned to her, their faces just inches apart.

"Stay here," he said. "I'm going out to take a look."

He heard the sharp intake of her breath, and then he pushed the storage room door silently open and crept into the dark kitchen.

But it wasn't entirely dark.

Cutter crept to the server window and slowly raised his head. There was ambient light coming into the diner from a slice of moon in the sky, and out in the parking lot a car's headlights were shining in through the full-length windows, filling the front of the diner with weird bright halos of light and strobes of movement and shadow.

Cutter saw two men. One was holding a crowbar. The other was holding a length of chain that was wrapped around the neck of a tall young woman. The woman's head was bowed and her hair hung down over her face. She was shaking and sobbing.

The man tugged on the chain, like it was a leash. He dragged the young woman across the room to a table. The girl went whimpering and cowered. The man slapped the side of her face with his open hand and her head snapped back.

"Move your ass, bitch," the guy growled. "This is happening, one way or another. It's up to you how it goes down."

The other guy laughed. He reached out for the girl's face and cupped her chin in his hand. "Not bad," he appraised her, holding her face to the light. She was tall and slim, with long red hair. The man's fingers slid down to the woman's throat and then continued lower. "You're our property now, bitch," the man's voice sounded like gravel in a cement mixer. "We own you. It's the new law of the land. We take what we want, and you put out when we tell you. You're ours to use until we find someone prettier. Until then you earn our protection by spreading your legs when we tell you. Got it?"

She was wearing a stained, dirty blouse and a dark skirt. The man's slid his hand down inside the open shirt collar. He felt the heavy weight of her breast through the fabric of her bra and squeezed hard.

The girl tried to recoil from the man's touch, whimpering in pain. She lashed out with her fist and struck the man on the side of the head. He laughed, but it was a nasty, vicious sound. "Seems like this one needs some training, Jed."

The guy holding the chain tugged hard and the leash bit into the tender skin of the girl's neck. She screamed out in pain and dropped to her knees. One of the men slapped the woman's face again and Cutter heard her begin to cry.

The men hoisted the girl up onto the table, spreading her out flat on her back. One of them forced her skirt up around her waist and spread her legs wide. The delicate fabric of the girl's panties was ripped away.

She struggled. The other man was standing over her, pinning her wrists. Her blouse was ripped open and her bra forced aside so that the soft pale flesh of her breasts swayed in the light as she struggled in impotent terror. The man lowered his head to the girl's writhing body and she screamed out in revulsion as his mouth covered hers.

Cutter braced the Glock on the sill of the serving window and took careful aim at the dark shape of the man standing between the woman's spread legs.

And then paused.

What could he hope to achieve?

What would he be risking?

For long seconds Cutter hesitated. Gunshots would bring any undead from miles around. And if he missed – and if the men had guns – the chances were that he would be killed. And then what would happen to Samantha? Would she suffer the same fate as the woman they were about to rape? Was he right to get involved in this?

The woman screamed again. The guy between her legs was unbuckling his jeans and forcing the girl's knees up against her chest. His face was a dark wicked mask of malice.

Cutter fired.

The sound of the bullet was enormous in the silence. It struck the man in the neck and he staggered. His expression registered a split second of utter disbelief, and then he crashed to the floor, gurgling and gasping in pain.

The guy who had the girl pinned down froze, and then whipped round in fear. He dropped to his knees and dragged at a nearby table for protection. Cutter saw the girl scramble to her feet, clinging at the shreds of her clothing. She stood, bewildered, in the middle of the floor, and her face was a pale white blob of terror and confusion.

The guy behind the table raised his head and looked towards the darkened kitchen where Cutter waited. Cutter fired again. The bullet went wide. The man ducked back down behind the table.

Cutter fired again, and this time the bullet was close enough to fill the guy with panic. He leaped to his feet and made a dash for the diner door. Cutter fired – not aiming for a specific point – merely aiming at the moving dark mass of the man's body as he reached the glass door and slowed to wrench it open. Cutter heard the bullet slap into the man's body: a meaty thump of impact. The man groaned and seemed to arch his back as though he had been bent backwards by some invisible force. His hand slid from the door and he spun around.

Harsh glaring light lit one side of the man's face. He was a brute: a big solid guy with a long dark beard and greasy hair. His face was contorted in pain. He was wearing some kind of a bulky dark jacket. Cutter fired one last time and the bullet struck the man in the face and killed him instantly.

For long seconds nothing happened. The silence came crashing down again like an anvil. Cutter kept the gun aimed and waited. He heard soft gurgling sounds coming from the body of the first man he had shot. The woman stood trembling and sobbing. Cutter could hear the soft clink of the chain around her neck.

Finally he came from the kitchen into the diner and went straight to where the man was slumped inside the door. Cutter kicked at the body with his foot. It didn't move. He went to where the other man lay. Cutter's bullet had torn into the man's neck. Warm wet blood gushed and pulsed out across the polished floor. The man had his hands clamped around his throat, trying to stem the flow. His eyes were wide and staring, fixed on the ceiling. Cutter let the man bleed out.

He went to the girl like he was approaching a startled forest animal. She was shaking feverishly, clutching at the shreds of her clothes. She backed away from him and her eyes were edged with madness and panic.

"It's okay," Cutter said softly. He reached out his hand for her. The young woman took a deep shuddering breath and then looked up into Cutter's eyes.

Cutter froze. He felt a sudden slide of disbelief. Shock jumped down his nerves and strung them tight. The girl's mouth fell open in dismay and recognition.

It was Jillian. It was the young woman who had offered her body to Hos in the bookstore basement in exchange for his protection.

Cutter gaped, and felt a sudden ghostly chill run up the length of his spine.

"Jillian?"

The young woman stared at him, and slowly the frenzy in her eyes dissolved. She nodded and Cutter saw the realization of recognition and relief pass across her eyes.

"Where is Glenda?"

Jillian looked down at the man who was slowly dying on the floor at her feet. "He shot her. She's dead."

Cutter recoiled. "And the other woman who made it to the Forester. What happened to her?"

"Dead," Jillian sighed. "They were waiting for us on the highway," she said softly. "They had motorcycles. They said we had to pay a toll to go any further..." her voice broke off for a moment and then came back steadier and calmer. "Glenda tried to shoot our way through. They killed her." As she explained, slowly Jillian dropped her arms to her side. Her breasts were full and perfectly rounded. She saw Cutter's gaze flick involuntarily down and she did nothing to cover herself. "They killed the other woman too."

"But not you?"

Jillian shook her head but didn't explain further. Cutter stared into her eyes. Something changed there, a challenge perhaps, or a flicker of resentment. He wasn't sure. She tilted her head and slanted her eyes so that her look was almost one of invitation and offering. "They brought me here – to one of the houses past the turnoff, but one of their bikes broke down on the way, so they found a station wagon," she turned her head towards the door, to indicate the headlights still shining through the plate glass windows. "When it got dark they brought me here for food – and for their fun, I guess."

The straps of her bra were broken. Matter-of-factly Jillian slipped the lingerie off her shoulders and tossed it aside. Her blouse hung open and she fastened the two bottom buttons slowly and deliberately, leaving a long deep V of bare flesh and cleavage. Then she scraped the hair back from her face until it hung back down over her shoulders. She stared at Cutter.

"You left us."

Cutter shook his head. "I took you as far as I could," he said simply.

"And then you left us. Why?"

Cutter thought for long seconds, trying to find the words to explain. Finally he sighed and said simply:

"Redemption."

At that moment, Samantha suddenly appeared in the kitchen doorway. She had the Glock in her hand and she came into the diner warily on silent footsteps. Jillian raised an eyebrow and glared at Cutter.

"Is she yours?"

Cutter frowned. He genuinely had not understood the question. Samantha spoke from the shadows. "I don't belong to anybody," she said.

She stepped into the light and lowered the pistol.

The two women studied each other, and Samantha's chin came up defiantly as she looked into Jillian's mocking eyes that were veiled with mystery and cunning calculation. They understood each other instantly – as though some intuitive charge of electricity had flashed between them. Jillian smiled politely.

"I underestimated you, Jack," she said softly, letting the ambiguity of her comment hang in the air.

The two women were about the same age, but there the similarity ended. Samantha was an inch shorter, and her body was lithe and athletic. Her breasts were small firm shapes against her shirt and her legs were slim and toned. Jillian's figure was more womanly with a deep flare from her narrow waist to her hip. Her breasts were larger and there was a more knowing and worldly sense about the way she held herself. It was as though Jillian had learned about the reality of life on the streets and grown into womanhood quickly. Samantha's child-like innocence made her seem almost awkward and gangling beside her.

Cutter glanced back out through the diner windows to where the station wagon's headlights burned bright and stark through the night. He made a snap decision. "We can't stay here," he said. "If there are zombies anywhere around, they'll be drawn to the noise and maybe the light. We've got to get away – now."

Samantha hesitated. "You said we shouldn't be on the road at night," she reminded him. "Jack, you said it would be too dangerous."

"I know," Cutter snapped. "But we don't have any option. Fetch the bag."

Jillian cut in suddenly. "We could use the house," she said. "The house the men took me to. It's just a mile or so along the turnoff."

Cutter paused. "Is it defendable?"

Jillian made a face and shrugged. "I... I don't know," she admitted. "It seemed to be. There were shutters on the windows."

"Did you see zombies?"

Jillian shook her head. "There were dead people on the street. I think the infection went through the area already."

Still Cutter hesitated. "Where is the house?"

"It's part of a small estate just up the road. It's the house on the corner as you make the turnoff."

Cutter looked at Samantha. He was filled with a sudden sense of inexplicable urgency. Samantha shrugged.

"Can you lead us there?"

Jillian nodded.

"Okay," Cutter decided. "We go and stay in the house until daylight. Then we'll double back to this turnoff and carry on north towards Eden Gardens."

Jillian clutched at his arm, and for a brief moment her wild fear returned and distorted her expression. "Will you take me with you tomorrow, Jack? I need to know..."

Cutter stared into the woman's eyes. Her expression was desperate and pleading. He glanced sideways at Samantha and opened his mouth to answer.

Then suddenly the night was ripped apart by the sound of a howling roaring engine and searching shafts of blinding white light. Cutter flung up his hand to shield his eyes and drew the Glock in the same instant, knowing with dreadful instinctive certainty that he was too late.

The night had just gone to hell.

* * *

Unseen dark shifting shapes were rushing towards the windows, thrown into sudden garish outline by the bright light. Cutter saw the shadows become silhouettes, and then hard undead forms. He swore. One of the ghouls slammed its bloody hands against the glass front of the diner and hissed with demented fury. Spatters of gore and dark slime from its mouth sprayed the window. Cutter recoiled. He drew Samantha and Jillian close to him as another zombie threw itself against the glass. It was the torn, mutilated figure of a woman. She was naked. Cutter could see the white bones of her ribs through a huge hole in her chest. She snarled at Cutter. Her mouth was filled with broken teeth and rotting putrid flesh, and her face was covered in ulcerated oozing sores.

Cutter dashed for the door and locked it. He looked around desperately for a barricade. "When that glass breaks we've had it," he said. "Sam, get ready to fall back to the storage room. We'll make our last stand there."

As he spoke, more undead ghouls shifted in the darkness, surging closer and becoming solid. The light was growing stronger and the sound of a roaring engine filled the night until the world became a swirling maelstrom of terrifying dark apparitions and deafening sound.

Cutter swung the Glock in an arc. Zombies were thick against the windows now. They were three deep, slamming their hands and hurling their bodies against the glass. Cutter could hear the terrible shock of each collision and knew that it must be just a matter of seconds before the windows shattered and the undead surged inside to kill them.

He backed away towards the kitchen, shielding Samantha and Jillian. Somewhere to his left, near the diner's entrance, he heard the sudden unmistakable sound of glass splintering....

Cutter drew one last deep breath and braced himself.

Suddenly a truck appeared from out of the night and crashed across the parking lot. It plowed into the mass of milling frantic undead bodies, cleaving a wedge through the zombies and cutting them down like wheat. The vehicle was lit up like a UFO. Banks of bright lights were mounted across the front grille and there were more spotlights fixed to a roll-bar behind the cabin. One of the spotlights swung around and blazed through the glass-fronted diner. The light blinded Cutter. He screwed his eyes shut and flung up one hand.

Sudden urgent gunfire filled the night, the muzzle-flashes of multiple weapons ripping through the darkness. The shape of a man leaped from the back of the truck and crashed the butt of his rifle against the door lock. The glass shattered, spraying in across the floor, and the door shook in its frame and then crashed back hard against its hinges.

"Get on the back of the truck!" a man's voice shouted in a broad Scottish accent, barking the order so urgently that the words sounded like they were almost joined together. "Now!"

He ran towards the group, a solid bearded man with short brown hair. He was wearing some kind of a thick bomber jacket and faded denim jeans. He grabbed Samantha and Jillian by the arms and hauled them towards the exit. Cutter scurried back through to the kitchen and seized the heavy bag. When he came back into the dining area, he could see the women being heaved bodily up onto the bed of the vehicle.

Cutter put his head down and ran for the door. He could hear the truck's engine howling, the big vehicle crabbing forward as though it were eager to be let off its leash. It was a 4WD with a long sided bed. It had monster rugged tires with a fierce jagged tread. Cutter saw several dark shapes crouched and covered behind the sides of the tray. They were directing short, controlled bursts of fire into the shifting undead figures, as time seemed to slow.

Cutter hurled the bag over the side of the truck and leaped. Strong hands caught him and heaved him aboard. The truck's engine screamed, then suddenly the vehicle was reversing backwards. Bright orange muzzle-flashes lit up the dark night, giving the scene a new flickering horror. The 4WD was surrounded by a mass of bodies that heaved and struggled and surged around the vehicle in a wailing undulation of skin-crawling horror. Cutter saw Samantha and Jillian curled up in one corner of the tray. There was a man standing over them, firing into the undead. Cutter drew his Glock and blazed away at two zombies who appeared out of the blackness, their faces pale and ghostly, and their fury like an insane frenzy. They hurled themselves at the side of the truck and Cutter hit the first one in the head and missed the second one completely.

Close behind his shoulder he heard someone grunt and then the undead ghoul Cutter had missed fell to the ground in an eruption of rotted flesh and shattered bone.

Dark snarling bodies clawed at the sides of the truck. Cutter saw one of the men aboard fire a rifle into a zombie's face and the thing vanished in a gout of brown gore and bone fragments. But another instantly took its place. The man beside Cutter lunged forward with the barrel of his rifle, jamming it hard into a contorted snarling face. The man grunted, throwing all his weight behind the thrust, and the muzzle went into the ghoul's eye. The eyeball burst as the zombie reeled away, flapping and twisting.

Cutter fired again into mass of dark clamoring bodies. A face appeared, staring up at him with malevolent rage. It was a man. He had a broad forehead and yellow slanted eyes. The man's face was covered with brown dripping slime. Half of his cheek had been ripped away, revealing jawbone, gums and teeth. The zombie snapped at Cutter hungrily. Cutter fired and somehow missed from point-blank range. He fired again and the impact of the bullet smashed into the zombie's skull and flung it backwards into the undead mass.

The truck kept reversing. Zombies flashed across the beams of light and disappeared again. The truck bumped and swayed over the undead and then slewed sideways. The big tires threw up a hail of loose gravel. The night filled with diesel fumes and smoke, and then the truck bounced up onto the road in a fishtailing skid. Cutter heard the crunch of gears and a sudden urgent whine as the vehicle leaped forward and raced back along the Draketown turnoff.

Cutter shook his head. His senses reeled, numbed and overloaded. The entire incident had taken no more than a few wild seconds, and had been carried out with almost military precision.

* * *

The 4WD pitched off the Draketown Road in a cloud of dust. Loose stones and gravel sprayed out from under the big tires as the vehicle veered sharply to the right onto the estate road. Cutter crouched down on his haunches and clung to the side tray to keep his balance. His eyes locked with Samantha's and he read the concern in her eyes.

Had they been rescued – or kidnapped?

Cutter wasn't sure.

The night was pitch black. Dark grey clouds had swept across the horizon, low and heavy with pending rain. Cutter glanced at the three men gathered around in the back of the truck. They were all heavily armed, and all wearing bulky clothing. They bristled with grim menace as their eyes hunted the night for danger.

The streets of the estate were deserted – the houses seemed dark and empty. There was litter strewn across the streets, eddying and swirling in the freshening breeze.

The 4WD skidded onto the driveway of a two-story house that had neat gardens across the front of the property and a low white picket fence.

Cutter looked around the side of the vehicle's cabin anxiously. At the end of the drive was a garage. The door was up. The truck parked up with a sudden lurch and the three armed men scrambled down off the back of the truck, weapons at the ready.

Cutter heard a deep authoritative voice barking orders as the truck's cabin doors swung open and slammed shut again.

"Mr. Knot, get that roller-door down asap," a man snapped. "Lone Wolf, take them inside and then get yourself upstairs. I want eyes on the road right now."

Men moved. There was a bustle of activity and Cutter found himself and the two women being escorted across a narrow concrete path to the back door of the house by the man with the Scottish accent who had burst into the diner. Behind them, the rest of the men followed, moving in concerted pauses as they swung their weapons in short covering arcs that swept the back fence of the home.

The women went in through the back door and Cutter followed. They were standing in a kitchen. The room was dark. Men spilled in behind them and then a light was flicked on. Cutter saw hard eyes and grim faces.

The man who had been giving orders in the garage gestured with his rifle, and the group went down a short hall into a living room.

"Back door, Mr. Knot," the man nodded to the guy who had lowered the garage door. "And lights out, please."

The guy called Mr. Knot was about forty years old – maybe an inch or two shorter than Cutter. He was a big solid man wearing jeans and a dark

179

jacket. His head was shaved and he had a lazy right eye. He was staring at Jillian. The thin material of her blouse gaped open so that the swell of her breasts and the hardened press of her nipples was exposed. The man shrugged off his jacket and handed it to the young woman wordlessly, then spun on his heel and disappeared back down the hallway.

The Scottish guy went stomping up the stairs at a run. He had a bolt-action hunting rifle fitted with a telescopic sight. Cutter figured the man had drawn sentry duty and imagined him kneeling at a bedroom window that overlooked the dark street.

"People call me Rampdog," the man who had been giving orders introduced himself. He was about Cutter's height, but twenty years older. He had steady calm eyes. He studied Cutter carefully, and then glanced at the two young women. He paused for a long moment, and then went to the living room window, his gait curiously awkward. The curtains were drawn. He snapped on a small table lamp and turned back to the group. He was wearing camouflaged combat gear and army boots and strapped across his chest was a canvas rig stuffed with magazines of ammunition. He reached down and rubbed at his thigh absently as though it ached. "This is Bob," the man introduced one of the others.

Bob was a giant: he stood head and shoulders above the others. He was wearing a chest rig over a dark shirt and jeans. The man nodded his head. He was older than the rest. He had a white beard, and he stared at Cutter with calculating intelligent eyes.

"And that's Underdude," the man said. "He's the kid. We call him UD. It's faster to say when shit is going down."

The man named Underdude smiled wryly and raised an eyebrow. "Hi," he reached out and shook Cutter's hand. Nodded politely to Samantha and Jillian. "Don't mind Rampdog. He's ex-army," he said, as though that simple fact explained it all.

It didn't. Cutter was hopelessly confused. He rubbed wearily at his eyes and sighed.

"Do I thank you for rescuing us, or do I hate you for taking us hostage?" Cutter turned to Rampdog.

"You thank us, dipshit," the man said. "We're not some redneck gang of desperados. We're a team. We saved your ass."

"And you're pissed off about it?"

The man's face turned cold. "I'll tell you in twenty minutes," he said bluntly and turned away.

"Bob," you've got the door. UD, you've got the window."

The other men moved into position. Samantha and Jillian slumped wearily onto a narrow sofa. Cutter heard the rhythmic snick of weapons being re-loaded. He swapped his Glock for Samantha's and then followed the man named Rampdog back out into the darkened kitchen.

"Anything, Mr. Knot?" the man asked quietly. The guy with the shaved head was leaning against the kitchen door, his body just a dark shape silhouetted by the soft light that filtered from the lamp in the living room. He was staring out through a gap in a heavily curtained window. He turned to Rampdog and Cutter saw the man shake his head curtly.

Cutter frowned. "Aren't we safe here?"

Rampdog turned on him, and although it was dark, Cutter could sense the suppressed tension that sparked from the man like a current of electricity. "This is zed-land, son. No one is safe. Nowhere is safe. All those zeds back at the diner haven't vanished into thin air. They're still out there somewhere," he snapped. "Hopefully we outran them and they've lost the scent. We'll know in a few more minutes. Until then, everyone is on alert."

Cutter nodded. "Okay," he said. "Where do you want me?"

Rampdog's eyes narrowed. He looked Cutter up and down. "Out of the way," he said bluntly. "You got caught in a diner, with no real weapons, no escape, and no way to defend yourself. It's hardly confidence-inspiring stuff. So why don't you just go back into the living room and keep the women company." There was a snarl of distain in the man's voice and Cutter felt himself bristling as his temper boiled over.

"I did the best I could," he defended himself archly. "And we would have been safe if two guys hadn't come to the diner to rape one of those girls."

Rampdog's expression didn't alter. "I know what happened. I saw it all playing out," he said. "We've been holed up here for twenty-four hours while Bob repaired the truck. We saw the two guys. They brought the girl to the house across the street. We watched them all the way to the diner."

Cutter stared in silence for a moment. "So you went there to rescue her?"

Rampdog nodded. "Like I said, we're a team, not desperados. We're men – not monsters."

The strain went out of Cutter in a long exhausted sigh. He was bone-weary and exhausted. Like a rubber-band drawn too tight for too long, he suddenly felt the heavy weight of lethargy crush down on him. He nodded at Rampdog and turned back towards the dining room.

In the doorway he stopped again and turned back.

"Thanks," he said.

Rampdog nodded but said nothing.

Because there was nothing more to say.

* * *

Cutter sat on the sofa beside Samantha and watched Rampdog prowl restlessly through the house for thirty minutes before he finally gave the order for the men at the front window and door to stand down.

"Take a break UD. You and Bob will relieve the other guys at 0400 hours."

The two men lowered their weapons and Cutter felt the tension in the room ratchet down.

Rampdog set his rifle down and went into the kitchen. When he came back he was carrying bowls of soup. He handed one to each of the women and then gave the last bowl grudgingly to Cutter. "We have a camp stove set up," he explained. "Eat. You look like you could all do with something warm."

The girls attacked the food ravenously. Bob and UD hovered in the background, relaxed, but ready. Cutter stared at the weapon Rampdog had propped in the doorway. He nodded.

"That looks like a hell of a gun."

Rampdog's expression didn't alter. He grunted. "It's a Bushmaster M4," he said. "Mr. Knot and Bob have the same."

Cutter nodded. He remembered the awesome firepower of the weapon and the way the zombies had been torn apart back at the diner. "Are you guys all ex-military?"

Rampdog shook his head, but it was Underdude who spoke up from the back of the room.

"Rampdog is ex-army," he explained. "He was a Sergeant with the First Cavalry Division. Did a decade in uniform, including a tour of Iraq. That's why we sometimes call him Sarge. The rest of us have different backgrounds." He gestured at the tall man who had stood guard at the door. "Bob here was a field technician for almost thirty years, and then taught himself computers. He's the team's mechanic and electrician. And he knows guns."

Cutter nodded. And then Jillian asked quietly, "What about you?"

Underdude shrugged. "I'm a gun guy," he said. "I load and sell ammo for a living – or at least I did until the world became over-run with zed's. I did a lot of security work. That kind of thing," he said vaguely.

Cutter frowned. "What about the guy in the kitchen?"

Rampdog shook his head wryly, and for the first time Cutter saw the hint of a mirthless smile break the across man's granite features. "Mr. Knot is part of the team, but he's a mystery," he said. "No one knows much about his background, and no one cares. He's good with a gun, and he's smart. He's a steady man to have around."

Cutter nodded, then glanced up at the ceiling. "And the Scotsman?"

"Lone Wolf ain't part of the team. Not yet, anyhow. We found him back in Draketown. He was holed up at a gas station, fighting off about a hundred zeds. We're giving him a ride south."

"Is that where you're heading?" Samantha suddenly asked, her brow furrowed with feminine curiosity. She moved restlessly on the sofa, and Cutter felt the warmth of her body against him.

Rampdog nodded. "The team is heading for Serenity," he said. "That's where we'll all meet up."

There was a brief silence. Cutter heard two muffled stomps vibrate through the ceiling. Rampdog glanced sharply up at Bob and the older man disappeared up the stairs.

Rampdog dropped to his haunches and stared at the group on the sofa like they were all gathered around a campfire.

"We're called Team Exodus," he said, his eyes drifting from Cutter to Samantha and Jillian, and then slowly back to Cutter. "We're a group of survivalists spread around the country who have been preparing for some kind of apocalypse for years. We're armed and we're organized," he said, and there was a touch of pride in the man's voice. "Right now we're on our way south to rendezvous with the rest of the team. Not everyone is going to make it – but everyone is gravitating towards a place that can be defended and where we can start again. We call it Serenity."

Jillian sat slowly forward, her eyes wide and almost mesmeric. "Where is this place?" she asked, her voice a subdued breathy whisper of sudden interest. "How far south is it?"

Rampdog had a folded brochure in his pocket. He spread it out on the floor. "It's a place called Biltmore Estate outside of Asheville in North Carolina."

The brochure was dog-eared and worn around the edges. The color had faded and flaked away along the crease lines and it was stained with sweat. Cutter looked carefully and saw a glossy picture of an elegant stately manor home set on rolling green fields and sculptured gardens.

Cutter narrowed his eyes. "What makes this place you're going such a good location?"

Rampdog folded the brochure and tucked it carefully back into the pocket of his fatigues. "It's an estate that was owned by a rich guy sometime in the past. Now it's a mountain tourist resort," he explained. "It's fenced in – and it's cold. In winter any zeds in the area will freeze."

Underdude had been listening on in silence. He broke away from the group and went to the window for a moment to peer cautiously through a gap in the heavy curtains. Satisfied, he turned back and came to where Rampdog was crouched. "Sarge forgot to tell you the best thing," Underdude added. "The estate has its own winery."

Rampdog nodded. "Yeah. It has a winery. I figure alcohol is going to become more valuable than gold in the new world. It's going to be currency."

Jillian held up her hand to ask another question as if she was in school. "How many people do you have heading towards this Estate?" she asked. "It sounds big. Surely you can't defend it between just the five of you."

Rampdog's expression tightened. He stared at Jillian for long moments of silence and his eyes became haunted. Finally he stood up stiffly and picked up the Bushmaster, as though the conversation was closed. He turned away, then seemed to change his mind. He turned back, and when he spoke again his voice was distant and disturbed.

"There are others," he said. "Other people like us. And our families."

"You have family?" Samantha asked.

Rampdog nodded. "My wife and son," he said, and there was a sudden heaviness in his voice that surprised Cutter. "Maria and Matthew. They've been in Miami for the past three weeks. They'll meet us there, if they are still alive. I've had no contact..."

"What about the others?"

Rampdog nodded. "Bob's wife and one of his sons work in hospitals. They may not have survived the first wave of the virus. But if they have, they'll join us at Serenity. We're going to need people with medical skills as we rebuild. And he has another son in Atlanta and a daughter in Boston. We don't know if they're alive or not."

At that moment Bob came down the stairs and stood tensely in the foyer by the front door. Rampdog went to him and the two men stood talking in quiet, urgent whispers for long moments. Cutter watched the men's faces and sensed their apprehension. It was in the way the men held themselves, the strain on their faces and in the hardness of their eyes. Underdude went over and joined the huddle. Cutter glanced sideways at Samantha. Her eyes were darkening as though she too had sensed an escalating alarm.

Cutter saw Bob retreat back up the stairs. Underdude drifted past them and disappeared into the kitchen. Rampdog came back to the sofa, his expression suddenly taut and focused.

"There are zeds out on the road," he said. "Lone Wolf has been tracking half-a-dozen of them.

They're coming back from the direction of the diner. They're drifting at the moment, and there aren't enough of them to bother us, but we're back on alert."

Cutter got to his feet and fumbled for his Glock. Rampdog put his hand on Cutter's shoulder. "We can handle this. We don't need you – but tomorrow these women will. So get some sleep while you can. That goes for all of you. At 0600 hours we're moving out of here. We'll get you back to the diner – and from there you are on your own."

* * *

Rough hands shook Cutter, and he came awake with a sense of heavy foreboding and unease. He sat up quickly. The Scotsman, Lone Wolf, was standing over him.

Cutter rubbed at his face. He felt as though someone had thrown a handful of grit in his eyes.

"Good morning, Sunshine," Lone Wolf said in a broad accent. He handed Cutter a small silver hip flask. "Drink up."

Cutter swallowed a mouthful. It was whisky. He felt the fumes scald the back of his throat.

"Mother's milk, that is," Lone Wolf said as he tucked the flask back into his pocket. "And you'll be needing more shortly. Mr. Knot has got some kind of stew warming on the camp stove. It tastes like shite."

Cutter stretched tight weary muscles. "What time is it?" The rest of the team was moving with silent purpose around him.

"Almost six in the morning," Lone Wolf said. "The sun's almost up, and we'll be on the move in about twenty minutes."

Cutter nodded. He reached over and gently shook Samantha awake. She had fallen asleep on the sofa, curled up like a kitten, with her head resting on Cutter's lap. She sat up slowly, her hair a messy tumble and her cheeks flushed. "Where's Jillian?"

Cutter didn't know.

"She's in the kitchen," Lone Wolf said. "She's been helping with the stew."

Behind them Rampdog stepped into the room. He came to where Samantha and Cutter were sitting. The Scotsman picked up their heavy bag and hauled it away towards the door. "I'll be putting this on the back of the truck for you," he said.

Rampdog watched the man leave.

"We move out in fifteen minutes," he told Cutter, his tone brusque and his manner business-like. "There were some zeds drifting past the house last night, but we haven't seen any more since. The plan is to get you back to the diner so you can be on your way. Did you have a car?"

Samantha nodded. "A little silver hatchback. We left it out front of the diner."

Rampdog nodded. "And do you have a destination?"

"North," Cutter said quickly. "Nowhere special. A town called Guthrie. Just a place about twenty miles north of the turnoff."

Rampdog clenched his jaw, but his tone remained level. "Fair enough," he said. Then he looked meaningfully back at Samantha. "If your destination isn't all you expect it to be, you can come and find us in North Carolina," he offered. "We're

189

heading down towards Newbridge today, and we'll push on further south from there. By the end of the week we'll be at Serenity."

For a long moment no one spoke. Finally Cutter stood up. He held out his hand. "Thanks for getting us out of trouble last night at the diner – and thanks for everything you've done for us since."

Rampdog narrowed his eyes in appraisal and shook Cutters hand. "You may just be competent," he said grudgingly. "I hope to God you are. I also hope you know what you're doing, because this girl is depending on you." The man turned for the doorway and then looked back over his shoulder. "Jillian is coming to Biltmore Estate with us. She and Bob approached me while you were sleeping and I said yes. He's a good man. He'll take care of her." Rampdog stomped out of the room without another word.

Cutter turned slowly back to Samantha. He wasn't sure if he was offended or relieved.

"Your choice," Cutter said. "You can go with the team if you want to. Jillian obviously feels safer with them than with me and I wouldn't blame you if you felt the same. I'm sure they have room for one more attractive young woman..."

Samantha's eyes narrowed and she glared at Cutter. Her whole posture changed, so that she thrust out one hip and put her hand on her waist. Her lips compressed to a thin pale line. "I'm not Jillian," she said coldly. "I'm my father's daughter. Don't expect me to give myself away like a cheap toy for the sake of protection. I'd rather die on my feet than live on my knees."

Cutter almost flinched. There was genuine anger and defiance in Samantha's tone that shocked him.

"We set out with daddy for the Garden of Eden, and that's where he would want me to go – and you're the man he wanted us to go with. So that's where I'm going."

Samantha and Cutter climbed aboard the back of the truck just as the sun was rising. Cutter shifted the black bag to a corner of the bed. Somehow it felt heavier. Lone Wolf, Underdude and Mr. Knot climbed onto the bed. Each man took up a firing position and re-checked their weapons.

Cutter looked around. "Where's Jillian?"

Mr. Knot gave a curt nod of his head. "She's riding up front," he said.

The 4WD came out of the garage at speed. Bob had his foot down hard on the accelerator and the truck bounced out of the drive onto the deserted street. Jillian was wedged on the bench seat in the cabin beside Rampdog, and the truck swerved and swayed from side to side on big springs as Bob set the vehicle to each corner without ever slowing.

They hit the open road and raced back towards the diner.

The sunrise was spectacular: a riot of orange and red that blazed across the landscape and spilled light over the dark shapes of night. The sky overhead was pale blue and clear. Cutter felt the fresh breeze against his face and glanced at Samantha. She was staring ahead, the wind tossing and tangling her hair and pressing the thin fabric of her blouse against the firm shape of her breasts. She caught Cutter's eye and somehow he read her expression as a challenge – maybe to be the man she saw him as – and to be more of a man than he saw himself.

Then she smiled, and it was so unexpected that Cutter found himself smiling back.

The truck veered off the road onto loose gravel and then skidded out front of the wrecked diner. The building was an empty shell. Broken glass littered the ground, and there were a dozen zombies lying still on the concrete, each of them with gaping huge wounds to their heads. The vehicle bounced and lurched over the bodies.

Bob braked hard and the 4WD slammed to a halt. Cutter and Samantha leaped off the back of the truck. Samantha went to the silver hatchback and looked inside the driver's side window.

"Keys are still there," she said.

"Get it out of the parking space," Cutter snapped. He felt his senses coming taut again and he crushed down on a rising tide of alarm. "Make sure it's running smoothly."

Samantha got the hatchback parked alongside the 4WD. She waved at Cutter through the windshield.

Underdude leaped off the back of the truck, hauling their heavy black bag. He flung it onto the backseat of the little silver car and then clambered back up onto the vehicle.

"Zeds," Lone Wolf pointed suddenly, but his voice was calm and detached. "Three of them across the road. Maybe a hundred yards away."

Rampdog heard the call. He got out of the cabin and stared back across the deserted street. He could see the zombies. Two of them were rotting filthy retches, hideously deformed and hissing with demented rage. They broke into a sudden sprint and raced towards where the vehicles were parked. The third ghoul was a big man who shambled unsteadily, as though newly infected. Rampdog made his decision.

"Put them down, Lone Wolf."

The Scotsman had his sniper rifle already up to his shoulder, tracking the zombies through the telescopic sight. He fired three quick shots, working the bolt of the weapon with smooth practiced precision, and the undead dropped to the ground before the final sound of gunfire had echoed and faded away into the still morning air.

"That will be the dinner bell for the rest of them," Rampdog turned to Cutter and frowned grimly. "It's time to go."

Cutter nodded. He stared past the shape of the big man and glared at Jillian through the open door of the 4WD. The girl had discarded the warm jacket so that she sat with her blouse gaping open and her skirt rucked up high on her thighs. She stared fixedly ahead through the windscreen.

She sensed Cutter's eyes burning into her but never turned her head. "I'm a survivor, Jack," she said. Her voice was empty of all emotion. "I know the game and I do what it takes."

Cutter stared. Said nothing.

Jillian's eyes swam with tears. "Don't hate me for wanting to stay alive."

Cutter turned away. Samantha was waving urgently at him through the windscreen of the hatchback. Rampdog got back into the passenger side of the truck and thrust his big hand through the window. "Be all you can be – and good luck to you both."

Cutter ran for the hatchback. Other dark twisted shapes were beginning to emerge from around the corner of the diner. Samantha spun the wheel of the car and put her foot flat down on the accelerator, heading north.

Heading towards Eden Gardens – and hope.

Six.
Paradise...

After a mile the road north narrowed to two lanes and the land beyond the thin ribbon of blacktop became rolling green fields of farmland.

Samantha relaxed her grip on the wheel and stole a glance at Cutter. He was watching her.

"You look like you're deep in thought," Cutter said.

Samantha paused, and then nodded. "I guess I am," she said. "But I'm thinking about a lot of things at once."

Cutter raised an eyebrow. "Such as?"

Samantha shrugged. "I was thinking how little I know about you... and how much I'd love to get out of these clothes right now."

Cutter looked at her sharply. There was just a trace of a twinkle in the girl's eyes – enough to suggest to Cutter than she was perfectly aware of the double meaning.

He glanced away and watched the farmland drift slowly past the window. There was a smudge of dark smoke on the eastern horizon. "I'm an artist," Cutter said at last. "A commercial artist. I painted book covers and CD covers – those kind of things for publishers."

It was Samantha's turn to be surprised. "Have you done work for any authors or bands I might know of?"

Cutter laughed. "Probably not," he said. He turned back and she was looking at him. He realized suddenly how young she was. Young and innocent. She had perfect smooth skin and big wide eyes:

impossibly beautiful and unprepared for the terrifying way the world had turned. But he knew too, that below that naïve exterior was a tough, steely resolve, and he found her beauty and bravery impossible to reconcile.

He shook his head, but for a different reason. "I don't think the books or music you listen to are the sorts of covers I'd be commissioned to illustrate."

She made a face, but it was a fun, lighthearted gesture, and then seemed to change the conversation completely.

"Tell me more about Eden Gardens," she said. She brushed a long golden tendril from her face with the back of her hand. "Tell me what you know."

Cutter sat back in the seat and closed his eyes. He remembered Hos and the conversation back in the bookstore basement. Had it really been just a couple of days ago? It seemed like an eternity had passed, so that his recollection was vague and halting.

"The man who told me about the place died back in Newbridge," Cutter explained. "But the night before, he told me he had a place in the country that was prepared for this kind of apocalypse. He told me he had been a survivalist for years –"

"– Like the men from Team Exodus?" Sam interrupted and Cutter nodded. "I imagine so," he said. "He seemed the type."

"Type?"

Cutter nodded again. "He had an interest in guns and tactics. That kind of thing," Cutter explained. "He told me his place was a fortress. He had a full collection of weapons and a stockpile of ammunition, food and water. And he said he had a generator."

Samantha smiled and her expression was almost dream-like. "Does that mean hot water for a shower?"

Cutter shrugged. "I don't know," he smiled. "Maybe. We'll have to be careful with water. But I remember the area around Eden Gardens being good farmland. So maybe it means we can plant a vegetable garden. If the land around the house is fenced or fortified."

Samantha slowed the car and diverted her attention quickly back to the road. There was a burned out vehicle across one lane. Thin wisps of black smoke still climbed lazily into the morning sky. Next to the car was the dark charred shape of a body. Cutter checked the Glock and wound down the window. "Don't stop the car," he said. "Pass the body on this side so I can get a clear shot if I need to."

Samantha obeyed. The car crept past at a crawl. The blackened body never moved, and as soon as they were past, Samantha built up speed again.

"Is it a big house?"

"What?" Cutter's mind was still on the remains that lay dwindling from sight in the car's side mirror.

"The house we're going to. The fortress. Is it a big house?"

Cutter frowned. "I don't know," he admitted. "But the man said he had come into Newbridge to try to rescue his mother. I think she was old, or ill. He never reached her in time – but that must mean the house has a couple of bedrooms at least. Maybe more, because storing six months of food and water, and weapons takes up plenty of space."

Samantha made a sound like a wistful sigh and then drifted into thoughtful silence once more "What do we do when we get there, Jack?"

Cutter frowned. "What do you mean?"

"I mean, what do we do?"

"We wait," Cutter said. "It's all we can do. We stay there until the virus burns itself out."

"Will it?"

Cutter nodded. "Eventually," he said. "It has to. The undead rise and they're slow, but they become faster as the virus reaches to all parts of their bodies – but they're still undead. They're decomposing. We've both smelt the stench. Their bodies are rotting away. Sooner or later, it has to reach the point where they are no longer a threat."

Samantha stayed silent, and Cutter felt compelled to reassure her in some way. "Or maybe the army will move in," he said. "If they have a good defensive line and the infection hasn't spread past the eastern states, then maybe they will mobilize the military and begin cleaning up. One way or another, this has to end eventually. We just have to reach Eden Gardens and wait it out."

As they drove on towards the town of Guthrie, the road gradually became choked with more abandoned cars, and more dead bodies. It became harder for Samantha to navigate the obstacles and keep the car on the road. She stopped the hatchback on a bridge and they got out cautiously and peered ahead.

The bridge was a rickety old timber structure that had been built back before the Second World War, when the farms and towns surrounding the city of Newbridge had all been linked by dirt roads. Cutter and Samantha went to the railing and peered down into the river. Bodies were floating downstream, rolling and floundering in the eddying water as it washed under the bridge.

"Where does the river go?" Samantha asked.

"The ocean," Cutter said. "It starts in the hills outside of Guthrie and winds its way south, past Newbridge and eventually runs all the way to the coast. In the old days, farmers used to send their produce to the city on barges."

Cutter went and stood on the hood of the car and swept his eyes carefully north and east.

The road cut through patches of woodland as it meandered towards Guthrie, and there were trees lined on both sides of the road. He squinted his eyes. There was smoke on the horizon.

He turned and looked south, and frowned.

"We must be almost there," he said cautiously. "The turnoff to Eden Gardens can't be much further. He pointed to the skyline. "There's smoke on the horizon, maybe seven or eight miles north," he explained. "That's most likely the township. And the turnoff to Guthrie is a couple of miles before you hit the town outskirts – so we can't be far from safety."

They climbed back into the car and Cutter got behind the wheel. There was an overturned Ford sedan blocking the road ahead and he was forced down off the road and into long grass to get past it. The Ford's roof had been crushed and he saw a small broken body trapped in the wreckage.

He drove on.

For some reason he had been expecting a big billboard sign by the side of the road with pictures of apple trees and beautiful gardens written in flowing italic script. The reality was very different. The turnoff to Eden Gardens was a small green sign with simple lettering:

'Eden Gardens 2 miles'

The sign had been peppered with buckshot so the paint had flaked and rusted around the impact dints. Cutter shrugged. He turned off the main road and the little hatchback bounced on its springs as the surface became a narrow dusty track that was grooved and rutted by years of use by heavy farm equipment.

They drove through a small grove of trees and then the land around them on either side of the trail opened up into lush farmland, fenced and furrowed into a huge patchwork of greens and browns. Cutter wound down the window and the air was fresh. There were mailboxes clumped in groups along the side of the road and more dirt tracks branching left and right towards isolated farmsteads that sat hunched in the distance, well away from the roadside. Samantha read off the numbers with a growing sense of excitement and anticipation.

"Twenty four and twenty six," she said. She pointed out through her window. One of the mailboxes was an old four-gallon drum. The other had been made of wood into the shape of a tiny house. Underneath was the name 'Rogers' painted in the big imperfect letters of an amateur.

Cutter drove on. The river followed them. It cut through the land like a fat silver python, reflecting the midday light and shimmering under the sun.

"Thirty," Samantha said suddenly. Cutter tore his eyes away from the river and glanced through the side window. Beyond the mailbox, he saw a dirt track leading towards a run-down clapboard house about two hundred yards from the roadside. There were a couple of rusted out trucks parked in front of the homestead and a post and wire fence leading all the way to the horizon.

Cutter slowed the car. Ahead was a rise on the ground, like the gentle undulation of a wave. He nodded. "Over that crest," he said. "The Garden of Eden."

Impulsively Samantha clutched at his hand and squeezed tightly. Her face was flushed and her eyes alive with hope and excitement. Her hand felt warm. Cutter didn't want to let it go.

He took a deep breath and checked the car's mirrors instinctively. There was a drifting haze of dust behind him from where the car had disturbed and kicked up dirt. Beyond the haze, the road was empty.

He took the car slowly up the rise and felt himself craning forward in the seat, anticipating the first glimpse of Hos's fortress that was to become their home together.

The hatchback went up the slope and at the top of the rise the lay of the land opened up before them. The river was to their left, beyond a quilt of green fenced fields, and narrow trails. And just off the road – maybe two hundred yards ahead – was a flat grassy strip of fenced-in land, surrounding an abandoned country church.

The church had a stone foundation and the rest was clapboard painted white, with three short timber steps leading up to solid wooden doors. The windows had been boarded over. It had a steep roof over the nave and a square tower with a bell.

Behind the church was a scatter of weathered gravestones, enveloped by a rusted wrought iron fence that wrapped around the edges of the property. The gates sagged open and tufts of long stringy grass grew around the support posts.

Cutter glanced at Samantha.

Samantha wasn't moving.

She wasn't breathing.

With a gut-wrenching sickening slide, Cutter suddenly realized why.

The car had rolled to a stop beside a mailbox: number thirty-four. It was Hos's fortress.

Cutter followed the trail that broke away from the road as it weaved a hundred yards through a tree-studded field and ended abruptly in front of the burned out blackened shell of a destroyed house.

The roof had collapsed, and the grass around where the building had stood was burned. Only one sidewall of the building remained. The rest had been utterly, totally destroyed.

Fifty yards away from the house was another burned out building. It might have been a barn – Cutter wasn't sure. He felt the crushing weight of total despair suck the breath from his lungs and drain away the blood from his face.

He stared, desolate, for long seconds, and there was the sound of a wild roaring in his ears.

Beside him, Samantha sat small in the shocked silence. She was weeping.

There was no Eden.

* * *

Cutter shook his head in disbelief, and then swore bitterly. He punched at the dashboard with his fist. He felt cheated – betrayed. He flung himself out of the little hatchback and stood staring at the ruined buildings.

Samantha climbed from the car, made small and quiet by her despair, and the force of Cutter's rage. She brushed at tears. High in the sky overhead, big black crows flew in lazy spiraling circles.

Samantha closed her eyes, and Cutter thought she might be praying.

He glanced away.

Then he froze.

The skyline was filling with hundreds of dark wavering shapes that seemed to rise up from out of the grassy fields beyond the burned out house. Cutter's eyes went wide in appalled horror. Zombies were cresting the gentle slope and beginning to spill down the fields towards where they stood.

Too many to count – a thick dark wall of snarling demented fury. Maybe still a mile away, but coming at them in a ragged serpentine wall.

"Shit!" Cutter spat. Samantha's eyes snapped open. She saw the terror in Cutter's face and followed the direction of his gaze. She went cold.

"Get in the car!" Cutter shouted.

He gunned the little engine and it roared to life. He crushed his foot down on the accelerator. The car leaped forward. The track was narrow, but there was open ground a hundred yards ahead. Cutter sped towards the clearing and as soon as the car had room, he threw the wheel hard over in a sharp turn. The tires skidded, biting into the gravel and then losing traction. Cutter felt a moment of weightlessness and the steering wheel kicked viciously in his hand. The motor roared. Cutter crushed down on the brakes. But it was too late. The hatchback went off the road and teetered on two wheels for a perilous split-second.

Then it rolled over onto its roof.

The sound inside the car was a crashing roar in their ears. The roof collapsed. Dust filled the air and the car – and Cutter and Samantha were slammed from side to side, and then hurled upside down. Cutter felt the Glock dig into his ribs and a flash of blinding pain. He heard Samantha scream out in panic and then his teeth bit deep into his lip and there was a copper-like burn at the back of his throat that tasted like blood.

Cutter groaned. The world was upside down. He kicked out hard at the crumpled door and crawled out onto the grass. Samantha was lying tangled, with her arm trapped between the seats. He hauled her out gently and wrapped his arm tight around her waist.

"Nothing broken?"

Samantha shook her head. "Your mouth is bleeding."

Cutter didn't seem to hear. He reached back inside the wrecked car for the black carry bag and found the revolver still in the glove compartment.

The zombies were closing quickly. They reached the burned building and swept down the hill unchecked.

Cutter looked around in despair.

"The river!" Cutter said. It was a few hundred yards away, down a gentle slope, directly away from the zombies. If they could get to the water ahead of the horde, they might be able to find a boat. He heaved the bag up onto his shoulder and the weight of it almost took his legs from under him. "Come on! Run!"

"No!" Samantha said suddenly. "The church!"

Cutter stared. "We can't escape. They'll be all over us. They'll pour in through that gate – or knock the fence down. It's abandoned Sam. It's a wreck!"

But Samantha had already started running.

Cutter staggered under the weight of the bag. The zombies were raging down the slope to intercept them. The church was still fifty yards away when Cutter realized the first of the undead would reach them before they made it to the church. Samantha realized it too. Cutter was behind her. Samantha was close to the wrought iron gates. She snatched the Glock from her jeans and dropped to one knee.

"Run!" she screamed at Cutter. He was sweating. His shirt was wet against the heaving swell of his chest. His legs felt like rubber. The bag was like a millstone around his neck. He felt his feet kicking up dirt as he staggered closer.

Samantha turned back to the closest zombies. There were two mutilated rotting shapes that had reached the shallow drainage ditch on the opposite side of the road. Samantha took careful aim and fired. The first ghoul was flung backwards into the grass. The second threw up its arms and snarled. Samantha fired again and the bullet hit the zombie in the chest. The ghoul spun round in a circle and fell into the dirt.

Cutter dropped to the ground beside Samantha. He threw the bag down in the dust and struggled up onto one knee. "Make every shot count!" he said. "We need to conserve the ammunition."

He fired at two more of the undead that were bursting through a low border of bushes on the opposite side of the road. One of them went down and stayed down. But the other got up, and Cutter had to fire three more times before he hit the ghoul in the head. He cursed.

"I'm almost out of bullets," he said.

Samantha snapped off one more shot and then ripped open the zipper on the bag and dug her hands inside. She snatched a look up at the zombies. They were twenty feet away. She felt her fingers fumble over unfamiliar shapes inside the bag and she glanced down.

"Cutter, there are boxes of ammunition in here!" she said in disbelief. And then her fingers felt deeper, and her eyes grew even wider. "And these!"

In her cupped hands she held three grenades. They were shaped like miniature pineapples. Cutter stared in wonder. "Team Exodus. The guys must have put them in the bag."

"What do I do?"

"Throw them!"

Samantha had sat through enough war movies to know the basics. She clamped one hand over the safety lever and pulled the pin with the other. Then she jumped to her feet and hurled the first grenade into the milling mass of undead.

She threw the grenade like a girl. It went twenty-five feet, wobbling in an awkward arc through the air, and landed amongst the zombies. Then suddenly the air was split apart by the sound of a deafening *'crump!'*, and the ground shook with the impact of the blast. Samantha was hurled off her feet. She landed on her back on the grass. When she sat up, shaking her head and her ears ringing, the air was filled with a swirling dust cloud.

"Did I get any?"

Cutter turned and glared at her. His face was covered in dust and there were clumps of grass and flesh in his hair.

"Give them to me!"

He took the second grenade and threw it high and long, and even before it had detonated, he had the pin pulled from the last grenade. The first exploded and he threw the final one at the same moment, tossing it into the closest of the undead who were clambering down into the muddy roadside drainage ditch. Cutter threw himself over Samantha's body, pressing her down into the grass and throwing his hands protectively over his head as the final grenade exploded and ripped the soft earth apart.

"Now run!"

They got to their feet and staggered towards the church gates.

Cutter didn't know if there were undead behind them, and he couldn't risk the split-second it would take to find out. He didn't dare to stop running. He knew if he did, he was dead. He pushed himself on with the last dwindling reserves of his will and strength until he was hunched against the sagging church gate.

The gate was wrought iron and eight feet high at its arched peak. It was about ten feet wide. Cutter dropped the bag and set himself the next task. The gate was rusted orange oxide and mounted on rusted old hinges. Cutter took a deep breath and threw his shoulder against the resisting weight.

"Get in here!" Cutter shouted to Samantha. She heard his voice and turned. "Try to find somewhere to hide. It's your only hope. These gates won't hold them. They're falling apart – and so is the entire damned fence."

Samantha ran back through the gate. There were zombies everywhere – a solid dark wall of rotting bodies. They pressed closer and the air filled with the stench of their decomposition. Cutter saw a hundred snarling spitting faces, each one hideous and ravaged and bloodied with demented mindless rage. He cried out and threw the very last reserves of his strength against the gate, just as the first of the undead spilled across the dusty road and began to funnel towards the opening where Samantha stood waiting like bait.

The gate moved. Not only moved – the gate swung effortlessly on whisper quiet oiled hinges. It swung in a sharp fierce arc and slammed hard against the post. Cutter's eyes went wide in bewilderment. He stood there staring down at his hands while the undead hurled themselves against the wrought iron. His hands were orange, but it wasn't rust.

He knew what it was. It was the one thing he *did* know about.

It was paint.

"Your belt!" Samantha shouted, her voice so full of panic that it cut through the fog of Cutter's confusion. He looked up. She was standing a yard inside the gate, near the post. Undead hands clawed through the wrought iron bars at her. She fired once into the closest zombie and the bullet ripped the top of its skull off. The ghoul slumped against the bars, held upright by the press of raging madness behind it.

Cutter snatched off his belt. He went to the gate post and handed his Glock to Samantha. She emptied the magazine into the milling undead, cutting a swath through the corpses so that Cutter could lunge forward and loop the belt around the post and gate fixture, sealing them in.

They stood back, face-to-face, with uncountable undead with just the church fence between them. The ghouls had spread along the length of the fence, shaking themselves against the iron bars and spitting thick brown gore until the slime of it covered the grass.

Cutter spun round quickly. Other undead were sweeping towards the side fence near the headstones. He watched them hurl themselves against the barrier and recoil in maddened frustration.

Cutter showed Samantha his hands. They were colored with dry paint dust, as if he had dragged his hand across the side of a house.

"It's paint," he said slowly, as the realization began to dawn on him. "I thought it was rust. I thought the fence – this whole church was an abandoned, ruined shell," he said. Then he shook his head slowly. "It's not. Samantha, it's Hos's fortress. He camouflaged the church and the grounds to look like it was abandoned and rusted out. It's all a mask."

Samantha stared down at Cutter' hands. She smeared some of the dry paint off and rubbed it on his shirt, then smiled up at him. Her face was pink, her eyes wide and wild with adrenalin and relief.

"Well if Eden was going to be anywhere, Cutter, then surely a church is the most fitting place in the world."

* * *

Cutter and Samantha patrolled the perimeter of the church fence for an hour before Cutter finally relaxed. It was solid. Under the mask of paint, the wrought iron was shiny silver, and the posts along the border were as thick as a man's wrist and footed in concrete. The undead threw themselves against the barrier in a relentless moaning wail of anger and frustration – and the fence held firm.

Cutter shook his head. "Hos hid his fortress well," he admitted. "He hid it where no one would ever think to look. In plain sight."

They couldn't force the front doors of the church: they were locked from inside and impossible to break open. Cutter went to the rear of the building. Under a small porch cover he found a second wooden door. It was bolted and hung with a heavy brass padlock.

Eventually Cutter ripped the boards off one of the windows and smashed the stained glass. He hoisted Samantha in through the opening and waited impatiently on the front steps for several minutes until the heavy doors were suddenly flung open.

Samantha was smiling.

"It's all here," she said, her voice a mingle of excitement and relief. "Everything we could ever need."

Built into the polished timber floor of the church was a square hatch, and beneath it a set of solid stone steps that led down into a dark Aladdin's cave. Cutter reached for the lighter in his pocket.

The area was about thirty feet square, with shelves lining each wall, divided and sorted – and even labeled. There were rifles and pistols and snub-nosed machine guns with boxes of ammunition for each. And there were the basics of survival: cartons of bottled water, rows of canned and dry food, water purification tablets and even packets of seedlings. There were tools and some basic farm equipment. And there was a generator alongside jerry-cans of fuel.

Cutter found a flashlight on a shelf and swept it around the room. The final wall of shelves was stacked with blankets and lanterns, pillows and sleeping bags.

Cutter went to the shelf and pulled two of the thick sleeping bags down. He offered one to Samantha.

"Where do you want to sleep?"

She took it with an impish smile, but there was something altogether more smoldering and womanly in her eyes.

She looked around them at the supplies that would give them life and hope in their new home – the new Garden of Eden – and she reached out for Cutter's hand and pressed it against the heat of her body. "Together," she said.

The End.

Made in the USA
Middletown, DE
20 March 2024

51795653R00119